STOLEN ROSES

de de Cox

Copyright © 2020 by de de Cox

STOLEN ROSES

All rights reserved. No part of this publication may be reproduced, distributed, or transmitted in any form or by any means, including photocopying, recording, or other electronic or mechanical methods, without the prior written permission of the publisher, except in the case of brief quotations embodied in critical reviews and certain other noncommercial uses permitted by copyright law. For permission requests, write to the publisher, addressed "Attention: Permissions Coordinator," at info@beyondpublishing.net

CREDITS:
Photographer:	Austin Ozier
HMUA:	Scooter Minyard
Assistant to HMUA:	Jeanette Moore
Location:	Jeff and Lisa Mumford farm
Female Model:	Savannah Dean Reeves
Male Model:	Bo Cox
Contributor:	Robyn Thomas / Twisted Sisters (a dear friend, fur baby mom of 3 (all rescues), and a Gemini who has the heart of a servant)

Quantity sales special discounts are available on quantity purchases by corporations, associations, and others. For details, contact the publisher at the address above.

Orders by U.S. trade bookstores and wholesalers. Email info@BeyondPublishing.net

The Beyond Publishing Speakers Bureau can bring authors to your live event. For more information or to book an event contact the Beyond Publishing Speakers Bureau speak@BeyondPublishing.net

The Author can be reached directly at BeyondPublishing.net/AuthordedeCox

Manufactured and printed in the United States of America distributed globally by BeyondPublishing.net

New York | Los Angeles | London | Sydney

ISBN: 978-1-952884-35-1

DEDICATION

There comes a time when we look back and see all the connections that God has brought into our life. Life moves us in different directions but sometimes it comes full circle. When I made the post about the fourth book, this very dear friend posted a pic and made a comment about what the fourth title should be. He was a dear friend of mine from high school. We went our separate ways as all graduates do. Adventures into college, jobs, and life. GOD brought us back to the circle. It will never be broken. My dear friend is happy. I am humbled and blessed that he and his husband are in my life. Pat Gary, you are a rock star. You are my hero because you were kind enough to share your vision for my dream. That's what true friendship is – supporting and dreaming with each other. Thank you for being you!!!

STOLEN ROSES

INTRO / PROLOGUE

Being on the road was not all that it was cracked up to be. Chasing a dream could be lonely. When she made the decision to leave her small town, a new chapter and journey was being written. He had made that decision easy for her. Time had passed, but the hurt and anger were still fresh in her mind. That day she walked into the barn four years ago, she thought he would be there, just like always. Ready to hold her tight and kiss her like he might never see her again. Something was dreadfully wrong. She felt it. She could not catch her breath. She walked inside the barn. She knew each step taken would change her life forever. The barn was empty. As she moved to turn around and run back out, she saw it. It was laying on top of the bale of hay in their stall where they had shared many afternoons and their desires and dreams.

A rose, her favorite flower.

He was the only one who knew this is where the most intimate of conversations had taken place. She reached and opened the note that had been laid with the rose. One tear formed in the corner of her eye and, then, another. She took the rose and crumpled it inside the note and stuffed it into her back jeans pocket. She walked outside and looked up to the heavens. Evergreen Colt would never forget this day. It would be seared in her mind for eternity. She made a vow right then and there to never return. She made a promise that no man would ever play with her emotions as he did. The name of Landon Dawson would never escape her lips again.

de de Cox

CHAPTER 1

Every time she walked out on the stage, fear enveloped Evergreen Colt. It had been like this from the very first time she walked through the tunnel and to the entry of the steps of her first concert. She could not put her finger on why she could not overcome stage fright. Once she walked up and heard the roar of the crowd, Evergreen became the #1 female country music artist that her fans had come to love and adore.

She stood still, positioned her guitar, pulled the mic down, and patted her back pocket to make sure it was there. Evergreen took one look at her band members. All nodded that they were ready. The song began, and the fans began to scream with excitement. This was the song she was known for in the industry. This was the song that had made her famous. This was the song that would keep her from ever trusting again. This was the song for him. This was "Stolen Roses".

The last set was finished. She looked into the audience and thanked them. She told them to have safe travels, God bless, and left them with her next concert date. Evergreen could feel the adrenaline rush. She was always aware of her audience and the genre she was playing to. She had taken one last look at her band and all acknowledged that the night had been a success.

Evergreen was physically and emotionally tired. As they approached the bus to settle in for the drive to the next venue, she would, at certain times during the evening, allow herself to think briefly, *I wonder where he is?* And, then, it was gone. He was gone. The day that marked Evergreen telling her mom and dad that she would be leaving to pursue her music career had been the worst and best day of her life. She would never forgive him. Her love and trust had been stolen by him, and yet, because of his leaving, she had found her true love: country music.

As she lay her head against the pillow, the sound of the rolling of the wheels placed Evergreen in a peaceful sleep. Sleep was needed. Rest was required. And again, *I wonder where he is?* were her last echoing thoughts.

The sound. What was that sound? Evergreen was in a deep sleep. All of a sudden, there was a loud thumping noise and, then, a bang, like a gunshot. Before Evergreen's eyes opened, she heard Gus, their tour driver, holler, "It's the tires. We've blown the back tires." Gus needed to get off the road as quickly as possible. Evergreen looked around to be sure that everyone was alert and knew what was about to take place. Everyone began to brace themselves for the impact. Gus was gripping the steering wheel with all the strength he could muster. The bus was swerving. The sooner Gus was able to get in the emergency lane and bring the bus to a halt, the safer all would be. Evergreen watched as Gus began turning off the interstate. Gus had been with the tour going on three years. He reminded Evergreen of her father. Gus had that special quality of just knowing when comfort was needed. He knew the entire band and crew by their first names. Evergreen felt safe with Gus behind the wheel.

She knew this incident was going to cause the tour to be delayed at their next gig. Gus had pulled safely to the side of the road and told everyone to sit still until he was able to review the damage. No use in everyone getting out of the bus until it was necessary. Evergreen grabbed her bag from the overhead. What time was it? She pulled her cell phone from the bag to view the time. It was 4:11 a.m. The band and crew needed to be at It's the Taste of Country Music Festival by noon. Not just to set up, but to walk out on that stage and play. This incident put Evergreen and crew in a real pickle. Evergreen needed to make a call to their manager, Will, so he could call the festival organizers and inform them of what had taken place. Could this day get any worse?

CHAPTER 2

Wow. What a week. Kids were coming out of the woodwork. Were there enough emergency rooms to accommodate everyone? As was his normal routine, Dr. Landon Dawson walked out into the emergency room waiting area and reviewed the lay of the land. It was an invasion of the sniffles, sneezing, and coughing – that's all he heard. It was going to be a long day and an even longer winter. Landon was known to the staff at Lullaby Children's Hospital as the one who was not afraid to walk around distributing a small toy to keep a little one occupied until his or her turn to be seen. Landon was also known as the charmer of the pediatricians at Lullaby Children's Hospital. Even the more mature folk were swept under his spell. He had a voice that commanded attention when he spoke.

As Landon made his way to the nurse's station to begin his rounds, his mind drifted back to the weekend and the beautiful brunette he had spent Saturday evening with. Dinner and a movie and, then, to her home for a bit of extracurricular activity. Landon did have a good time. But there had been no spark to pursue his interest to ask her if she'd like to go out again. He thought of his romantic interests over the past four years. In reality, there had been none to speak of. The friendly get-together with hospital staff and the occasional holiday events, but no one could replace what he had left behind.

Love.

Love was something like the clouds in the sky before the brightness of the sun shone. The love he had shared with her could not be kept hidden. Both their families had seen the closeness since Landon and

Evergreen were small children. As Landon pondered his rounds, he took a trip back down memory lane.

She had been his sanctuary. She had been the sunshine in his heart, even on the rainy days. The farm that Evergreen and her family lived on had taught both Evergreen and Landon discipline and education, sometimes more than the school setting. There was much to keeping a farm going. As soon as Landon had eaten breakfast on the weekends, he would holler at his mom that he was headed to Evergreen's. Landon's mom could peek out the door and watch Landon ride his bike down the road a bit until he made the turn into Evergreen's home. The mornings were the best. He rode his bike up to the porch and laid it on the ground. There was not time to put the kickstand down. Just as he would get ready to knock to see if Evergreen was up, she would appear with a smile on her face. Landon thought she looked like an angel. There was always a bounce in her step, and she would never stop talking about what they were going to do. Landon learned that she was so full of enthusiasm for life that she just could not stop talking. He loved listening to her and what she dreamed. From the very first time that Landon and Evergreen sat on the bale of hay in the stall, there was an attraction. It was undeniable.

Landon and Evergreen would rush to slide the barn doors closed. The only sound you could hear was Leroy, her pet cow, at the other end. It was as if Leroy knew he needed to stand guard. No harm would come to them, so long as he was on watch. Landon and Evergreen would talk for hours about what they wanted to be when they grew up. Evergreen desired to be a country music artist. She wanted to travel the world and share her passion of songwriting, as well as singing on the Grand Ole Opry stage. Landon knew he wanted to be a doctor and work with kids. When he was young, he had asked Santa for a doctor's kit – the kind that was black and was built like a briefcase and could hold all the surgical supplies needed. That Christmas was one Landon would never forget. The medicine bag was attached to Landon's hip. Every chance he got, he would take a family member's temperature or give them a pretend shot in the arm.

This was their haven. This was their spot. No chores needed to be done. They were alone with each other. Landon and Evergreen had become inseparable. As time passed, their tightknit friendship had blossomed into something more. Evergreen knew that her heart would beat faster and her breathing changed. She could only chalk it up to the plain and simple fact – it was love. From the very first time, when he had brought her the white rose, Evergreen had placed all in her small hope chest. Each rose had been gently laid in a handkerchief, and, then, the date was written in marker and folded away. This was Evergreen's favorite flower. Landon had told her that a red rose whispers of passion, but the white rose breathes love. Little did Landon know the one single white rose would become a treasured memory.

CHAPTER 3

"Dr. Dawson", he heard one of the nurses call his name more than once. "Would you like to go to a concert with us this weekend? We have an extra ticket. It's EC and Daybreak playing. It's the Taste of Country Music Festival. There are several opening acts, and, then, EC and Daybreak are the main group", Rikkie Dade, the director of nursing, asked. Landon thought to himself that he did not want to spend the weekend alone. He could fly to his Florida home just to get away, but he knew he would not enjoy just two days and, again, he would be by himself. *Why not*, he thought. What could happen at a little country music festival?

He looked at Rikkie and replied, "Sure, just leave me a note at the nurse's station, with all the details, and I will meet you guys." Rikkie watched as Dr. Landon Dawson walked down the hallway to his first patient check-in. Dr. Dawson was an enigma to most everyone at Lullaby Children's Hospital. He kept to himself a lot, but was never unkind. Just by looking at him, he exuded power and respect. He was one of the most highly sought pediatricians at Lullaby Children's Hospital for childhood cancer. He did not mince his words. He did not lie to a child. Dr. Dawson's take on telling the truth, no matter how serious, was that the patient deserved to know and to be well-informed and educated on the diagnosis. There was no need to leave anyone in the dark. The staff admired this quality and his integrity. As the director of nursing, Rikkie knew this was true. She had seen and observed it firsthand.

Rounds were done, and Landon was headed home. He made it to the front door, and, then, he remembered the concert. Rikkie was to have left a note regarding the concert at the nurse's station. He did not feel like waiting on the elevator, so up the steps he jogged. He hit the button that would allow him access to the sixth floor pediatric wing. He was out of breath when he arrived in front of the nurses' station. Two of the nurses looked up, immediately thinking an emergency was about to take place.

Lucy inquired, "Dr. Dawson, are you okay? Can we help you with something?"

Landon smiled and laughed. "Lucy, I'm fine. I just forgot the note about the concert this weekend. Did Rikkie leave a note with details for me?"

Lucy could not help but shake her head. "Don't ever do that again, Dr. Dawson. You had us worried. And yes, it is right here. She told me to tell you, 'no excuses.' We will see you there, yes?"

"Yes, Lucy, you will. I promise." As Landon tucked the note safely in his pocket of his scrubs, he winked at Lucy and told the crew to have a blessed evening.

The drive home was longer than usual. Landon had an uneasy feeling about this weekend and an even more uncertainty about attending the concert. He had never heard of the band that Rikkie had mentioned. Festivals were really big in the community. Vendors, food, arts and crafts, pageants, country music bands – all made the festival a success. It was a community and family affair. May be this would be what he needed. Just a night with friends. No expectations. No commitments.

CHAPTER 4

Landon pulled into his driveway and parked. He walked up to the front porch, put the key inside the lock, and began to turn the key, but the door was already open. Someone or something was in his home. He looked around with caution. Maybe he should try to walk without making a noise. He chuckled. Yeah, right, a 6'3" 200-pound guy trying—or at least attempting—to be another burglar. His younger sister, Willow, had decorated his home from top to bottom as Landon had requested. She had the "touch". Landon could not see, but he sensed that something was amiss. In the corner was the umbrella rack Landon used for his baseball bats. That was another story how that usage came about. All Landon knew was he needed to grab one and be ready to swing.

As fast as lightning, Landon grabbed the bat. Landon was trying to adjust his eyes to the dark when he saw her exit the bathroom and stroll right towards him. She leaned up to kiss him on the cheek. She told him hello and that he was late. He positioned the bat standing up, since there was not a threat any longer. He could throttle his little sister right now. *How in the world did she get in? Where had she gotten a key? How long had she been there?* Questions he wanted answered.

"Willow Rainey Dawson, you're dang lucky I didn't swing that bat," he said.

Willow laughed. "You're all bark and no bite. You had to know it was me. Didn't you see my car? Oh wait, you can't see my car, it's in the back. Oh well, at least you didn't hurt yourself. Oh, and one more thing, big brother, you gotta hide your keys better. I knew they would be in the bucket, under the stone, hidden by the plastic bag. Remember, that's what mom and dad did, so they knew where a key would always be for those 'just in case' times."

Landon looked at his little sister, "Am I to assume this was one of those 'just in case' times?"

"Absolutely, why else would I be standing here with you?" stated Willow.

Landon reached and pulled her into a big hug. He loved his only sister. For the life of him, he could not remember if Willow had called to tell him she was coming, or if she just decided to surprise him. Either way, he enjoyed spending time with her. She had left home and pursued her dreams. She was independent and exuberant about life. She had placed her mark on the interior design industry and was sought after for her expertise. To say he was proud was an understatement.

"Okay, what happened? Why are you here? What's going on with you?"

Willow smiled. "Nothing big, just checking in on you. How's life? How's work? How's the love life?" There it was. Landon knew what she was up to.

"Still the same, Willow. I work a lot of hours. I come home. I rest, and, then, I hit the sack and back up at it again. Nothing unusual. I guess you could say I'm just dull and boring."

Willow shook her head back and forth. "Try again. That doesn't tell me anything. Have you heard anything from her or about her since you left?"

Landon had often wondered in the first year of leaving if he had made the right decision. He had returned several times to see if she was still there, but there was no sign of her. He dared not go back to her parents' home, for fear of what she may have told them. He loved her parents just like they were his own. She was an only child and Landon knew that as soon as he made the decision to leave, they would not be pleased that he had hurt their daughter. As a matter of fact, Landon was pretty sure they would consider him pond scum after the note he had left.

Landon did not want to discuss "her" anymore. Willow looked at him and asked, "You're still sure that you made the right decision?"

Landon replied, "There was no right or wrong decision. It was what was needed to take place in order for both of us to do what was necessary."

"Yeah, yeah," Willow said. "Tell me that you don't think about her and where she is and what she is up to, and I'll drop the conversation."

Landon had thought about her more than he needed. He had made several attempts when he had driven back home to speak to the locals to see if they had heard anything about her. She had not returned for over a year. Folk just assumed she had moved on with her career and her life. Landon looked at Willow and said, "I do think about her, but thinking of her will not get anywhere. Anything else we need to hash over?"

"Say it," Willow implored him. "Admit it." Sometimes, Willow was like a dog with a bone. She just would not let it go.

"Yes, Willow. I think about her, but Evergreen Colt is not a part of my life anymore. Satisfied? Can we fix a bite to eat now?"

"Whatever you say, brother. Whatever you say."

CHAPTER 5

Landon had rested better than he had in the past week. He enjoyed when Willow came to visit. He genuinely adored the time they spent together. Bantering about her career and best of all, her new love interest, his best friend, Dr. Silver Bleu. He entered his kitchen and could tell she had already re-organized the kitchen (it was in her blood, she just had to touch and fix).

"Good morning, little sister," he greeted her as he watched her decorate the table with placemats and napkins.

"Good morning, big brother. Why were you hiding these beauties? They just make the table shout WELCOME HOME!"

"To be honest, Willow, I did not know I even had them. It's just a table." Landon knew that would get her goat.

"Not even going to bite today," Willow told Landon and punched him.

"What's on tap for today? It's the weekend. It's Saturday. Let's do something before I have to head back," Willow suggested.

"Let me make a phone call to Crispin to see if he's going," Landon said. "The Taste of Country Musical Festival is taking place today. If you have time, why not just stay and attend with me and the rest of the staff from the hospital?"

Willow did not have to leave until Sunday afternoon. She loved country music almost as much as Landon did. "Sure, why not? I have not been to a festival since Silver and I attended Blessing's big country music festival."

"Great," Landon told his little sister. "Let's shower and then shake. The concert begins around noon. The main act, from what Rikkie told me, is the EC and Daybreak Band."

"Done," Willow agreed. "Give me an hour, and, then, we'll head out." Landon did not know why he was excited that his little sister would be attending with him, but he was glad she had made the decision to do so.

"One hour, my tuchas," Landon looked at Willow as she finally emerged from her bedroom.

She laughed. "Sorry, I didn't realize how long I had been in there. Let's do this. I am actually anxious to hear this band and, of course, to see the craft and food vendors."

As they locked the doors behind them, Landon said "I'll drive. We'll put the top down, since it's so warm, and the sun just adds to the day."

The travel time to the festival was not too bad. Now, just to find a parking spot. Everyone from the town of Hopeulikit, GA was in attendance. Families, including dogs on leashes and small children, were walking the middle of the streets, so they could observe booths on both sides.

Landon had received a text earlier that morning from Crispin that everyone would meet around 11:45 a.m. and, then, head to the pavilion, where the featured band would begin playing. Landon turned to see Willow looking at a jewelry booth. She loved unique specialty items that were out of the ordinary.

"Come on, or we will be late meeting everyone," he hollered at Willow. "We will come back, I promise."

"Always Mr. Punctual, aren't you? Have you ever been late to anything dear brother?"

"Nope, and I'm not going to start today. Hop to it."

Landon loved seeing the community milling about. The day was breathtaking. So much to see and do. Could they cover it all in one day? Landon spotted Rikkie and a few of the other nurses from the pediatric wing of Lullaby. They were laughing and hugging one another hello. They saw Landon and hollered for him to make his way to them.

When Landon stopped in front of them, Rikkie commented, "Well, I never thought I would say this, but 'real men' *do* wear pink." Landon had not thought twice about the pink Henley shirt he had decided to wear. He actually did like pink.

"Okay, enough, he told Rikkie, "I still have a reputation to protect."

"That you do, Dr. Dawson, that you do." Rikkie began counting everyone, just like a teacher calling attendance in school, and then looked at everyone. She locked arms with Landon and Willow and began moving forward. With that one step, Landon's friends knew to follow suit.

When they approached the pavilion where the band was to play, they were a bit surprised that it was packed—and packed rather tightly—with folks waiting to hear The EC and Daybreak Band. You could see smiles on the faces of those waiting. The emcee for the day came out. He tapped the microphone twice to capture everyone's attention.

"Folks," he started, "it seems there's been a bit of a delay with the featured band. I received the phone call early this morning that they had two flat tires and did not know the exact time they would be arriving. We do know that they should be arriving here shortly. If you can just give us about 10-15 minutes, we should be ready. Remember, we have vendors who are ready with lemonade, elephant ears, hot dogs, cotton candy, and all the sugar needed to get you excited about the festival. We do not know when they will arrive, *but* we *do* have some entertainment for your pleasure."

Everyone cheered. The emcee turned to look over his shoulder and acknowledged whomever it was behind the stage. He turned back to the audience and with exuberance, he stated that the featured band had just pulled into the pavilion parking lot. "Let's give them a few moments to get the sound check and equipment situated, and we will get right back with you." Landon and the crowd watched the band do a quick methodical sound check.

Landon saw the emcee walk towards the back of the stage and begin to speak with several members of what he assumed were EC and The Daybreak Band. The emcee nodded in agreement with one of the band members, turned straightway back to the microphone, and told the packed crowd to put their hands together and welcome EC and The Daybreak Band.

The crowd began with thunderous applause, and so did Landon and his friends. Everyone was screaming. All had their hands waving in the air as each band member took their rightful spot on stage. The lead guitarist approached the mic and said, "It is our extreme pleasure to be here with you guys and to begin the weekend kickoff of the festival. And now, please welcome EC, our songwriter for the band, as well as our lead vocal."

Landon was watching as the young lady began walking towards the front. He was not close enough to see her until she hit the middle of the stage with the mic. She had her guitar strapped across her. She grabbed the mic and stated, "Good evening, I am EC – Evergreen Colt. The Daybreak Band and I are happy to kick off the festival. Let's get this party started!!!"

Landon did not hear anything after the words "I am EC –Evergreen Colt." This was not her. It could not be her. This was not the little girl he had shared his hopes and dreams with. This was not the teenage girl he could not wait to meet in the barn in their special stall. This was not the young woman he had left the note and white rose on the bale of hay. Landon's heart was racing full throttle. He had begun to break out in small beads along the sides of his face. He looked up, and standing before him was the most exquisite woman he had ever laid eyes on. Landon could not stop staring.

She was even more beautiful than the day he had left. She was dressed in a beautiful gold velvet slip top, jean jacket, bell bottom blue jeans, and cowboy boots. She pulled the guitar in front of her to position it and pulled the mic towards her lips. He wondered if they were as soft as the first time he had kissed her in the barn. And then, it happened. She looked right at Landon. She didn't even blink an eye. She didn't even miss a beat with beginning the first song of the set. As she began to sing, the crowd was moving closer to the stage, and Landon was moved with his friends as they did the same. The closer he moved to the stage, the more definitive were the words of the song. Landon heard the first few words. They were of love and stolen roses, and he knew. The song that EC and the Daybreak Band were singing was of that day. The day he had left the note and the rose. The song was deep with emotion. Evergreen stopped playing the guitar and grabbed the microphone with both hands. The words of hurt emanated from Evergreen's voice. You could see a few of the girls wipe their fingers near their eyes to wipe away the tears that they hoped no one would see. For the entire length of the song, Landon watched each movement that Evergreen made on the stage. As she worked the stage, she made sure to include as many as she could. As the song came to its conclusion, Evergreen stopped in the middle of the stage. Her eyes were directed at Landon. He felt the sensation of the daggers directed towards him. Evergreen stepped back from the microphone and told the crowd she would return. The Daybreak Band would be bringing 80s hits their way. She turned and left the stage. Landon could not see the direction she went as she took the steps down the back of the stage. He needed to see Evergreen. He just wanted to… well, he didn't know exactly what it was he wanted to do—say hello?

CHAPTER 6

Evergreen and the Daybreak Band were elated they had made it to the festival in time. The stage had already been set. The only issue was to do a quick sound check. They hated to do that while the crowd was already in attendance, but it was necessary. Evergreen, from the corner of the stage, did a last-minute check of the guys to be sure all was set to begin. Each band member gave her that "special" wink. They were ready.

Evergreen had paid her dues in the industry. She had been travelling and playing for the last three years in small honky tonk dives. One of these venues was where she had met her current agent/manager, Will, who was also her boyfriend. He had approached her after her set was finished and asked if she needed something to drink and if she had time to meet with him regarding her career and next gig. Evergreen agreed, but the meeting would be in the venue where she was playing. She did not drink alcoholic beverages, but was always intrigued to hear the "spill" of talent agents. As the conversation progressed, Evergreen had to admit she was entertained by the information relayed. Will told Evergreen he would take her out of the honky tonks and place her in venues that were of immense size and far-reaching into all genres. Evergreen had informed Will that she would need to speak to her band and get their input and insight on the details given. Within two weeks, EC and The Daybreak Band had been formed and created.

Evergreen's intuition told her that Will was good folk, as her grandma would say. She trusted that he had her and the band's best interests at heart. Will had followed through on every promise made. Evergreen's career had taken off. She was in the top 20 country music artists. Her song that she had written, "Stolen Roses", had debuted in the top 25.

Evergreen's life was just as it should be. She had followed her dreams and had become a successful singer/songwriter. Everything and everyone had been moving in the direction that would place Evergreen on top of the world. Until today. Until just a few moments ago.

Evergreen was pleasantly surprised. The stage, the sound, the lighting and mics were set. Every time she walked out to take the stage, butterflies would begin in her stomach. This set the tempo for her opening set. There had never been a time that she did not feel nervous taking the mic and beginning the concert.

She loved looking out into the audience and seeing the anticipation of them waiting for that first note. Today, because of the incident with the van, she had felt rushed, but knew they could pull it off. Evergreen and the band had been in worse situations with delays in getting to venues. With her new song, "Stolen Roses", climbing the chart, Will had encouraged her to open with it. PR and marketing played such a part in the success of any debut. She had written the song with her entire being. Evergreen had not only written from her heart, but she had written from her pain. The pain of losing the most precious gift that could be given to you – the gift of friendship and the gift of love. It had taken a year for Evergreen to be able to control her emotions of betrayal. In the end, she figured she might as well write a song about it. That day would forever be etched in her memory.

Evergreen and the band were on that natural high of rushing around and positioning themselves. The crowd was chanting her name – EC, EC, EC. Using just the initials of her name had also been a huge branding ploy, and it was working. Unless you personally knew Evergreen Colt, you would not know it was her unless you stood face to face with her. She and the band made it their mission that not only would the fans in the front be focused on, but the ones who stood in the back would also receive the same kind of attention.

As Evergreen began the song, it was in her nature to take the mic and welcome everyone and peruse the crowd. By doing this, Evergreen could assess the temperature of the crowd. She grabbed the mic to extend towards her and pulled her guitar around to position it. She had placed the pick in her hand. She looked up one last time to acknowledge the crowd and the band's readiness, and then she saw HIM. Only she could not tell for sure if it was him or a figment of her imagination. Oh yes, there had been plenty of times when something would take her back to the barn and all the treasured memories of her youth. Even more so, there were times on stage that a song would take her back to the pain of finding the note. That was one more item that she had kept reminding herself to never allow love to be given so freely. She had built the walls around her heart to protect her. She reached in her left back jean pocket to be sure that it was still there. It was. The note she had found that day with the rose that would change the direction of her life. She had memorized the words written in his handwriting. She brought her hand forward and began the song she had written as a stronghold. She poured her heart out to the audience. Evergreen could tell they were affected. There were several women who had wiped the tears away, looking around to be sure no one had seen them.

After Evergreen finished the song, she knew she needed a few seconds to collect herself. Evergreen could not believe he was there. What were the odds? A trillion to one. Her first initial thought was, *Does he know its me?* And her second thought was the plain and simple fact she would like to slug him and ask him the burning question: Why? Why did he leave?

She exited the stage with haste. Evergreen could not breathe. It was as if life was being taken from her. She stopped behind the stage where an entry – exit had been placed for the band and for the band only. She bent down and placed her head in her hands. Evergreen needed to regroup her thoughts. She knew there were several more songs that the fans would be expecting. Then, she heard the words from the man whose name she had promised herself she would never utter. "Evergreen, it's Landon. Are you okay?"

Okay? Was he joking? No, she was not okay. He was standing there in front of her. He was standing in her way. He was *her* Landon. The feelings she had hidden for so long were surging forward, and she did not think she would be able to stop them. "*Okay*...am I *okay*? Of course I'm okay—why wouldn't I be?"

Landon did not expect the seething sting of her words. He truly was worried when he found her holding her head in her hands. Landon had not expected the animosity that was emanating from Evergreen Colt. "Yes, I am fine. Go back with your friends and enjoy the rest of the concert. I was on my way to get my other guitar. In our haste to get the stage set, I forgot." And just like that, she turned to walk towards the parking lot with haste. She did not even dismiss or acknowledge his presence. Landon knew this was night was not going to end well. He would talk to her, and she would listen.

Evergreen made the excuse of the forgotten guitar so that he would leave. Evergreen could not even utter his name without her face turning blood red. Of all the questions he could ask her, that was the one. Geeze, if she had the time, Evergreen would have given him a piece of her mind and then some. Evergreen knew she had to return to the stage. She could hear the band closing out the last song and, then, she would be up next to follow with the next set of songs to finish the evening.

She turned to make sure he was nowhere in sight. *Good*, she thought. *Let's finish what I came here for: to sing for my fans.* As Evergreen took the stage, she took a quick glance into the audience. Evergreen could see the group that he had been with, but he was not with them. Maybe he just took the hint and left. Evergreen did not want to see him. Not now. Not ever.

CHAPTER 7

As Evergreen left with the ruse of getting another guitar, Landon knew she was lying. She was a horrible liar when she was younger, and she still was, even after all these years. He chuckled to himself. He still knew her. He would see her, and it would be tonight. There was a lot to discuss and issues that needed to be resolved, whether she liked it or not.

Landon did not want to go back to his friends, and especially not to where his little sister would be, with no fewer than a 1,001 questions to ask him of his whereabouts. He had no desire to be caught in the middle of the group, with no escape and even more so to have to answer questions as to why he had left their company for the past 15 minutes. He would wait. He was a man of patience. He always got what he wanted, and right now, he wanted an audience with Evergreen Colt.

As Evergreen thanked her fans and the festival committee for the evening, she broke into her last song of the set. This entire day had been one for the books. There was just no way she could have foreseen or even made up the day's events. She was ready to catch upon some much-needed rest. The band and Evergreen came to the front of the stage, waved their goodbyes, and then exited one by one. All were pumped and stoked about how the audience reacted, not just to "Stolen Roses", but to the two new additional songs that had been debuted. This was good. No, it was *great*. Evergreen heard them talking to each other and rating how well the event finished. She loved her band. Each one complimented the other. All of The Daybreak band could sing. All could play multiple instruments, which helped when needing to lay down tracks for a new song. Evergreen was thrilled that they were so ecstatic over the concert. Evergreen knew the next gig was even bigger than this. She needed the guys to be on a natural high and to take it with them as they travelled throughout the night. Evergreen began her descent down the steps that would take her back to the tour bus. She needed seclusion to escape her emotions.

As Evergreen was about to turn, she felt it. It was him. He was standing there smiling. That was it. This was all she could handle. Where the courage came from, she had no idea. She walked over to Landon Dawson and pointed her finger at him and said, "Don't, whatever you are going to say, it ain't gonna work, I got your message loud and clear—or should I say your note."

Landon watched as she exited the stage. *Good lawd*, she was beautiful. The best word that came to his mind was "striking". She was even more breathtaking than the day he left. And she was even more fit-to-be-tied than what he could imagine the day he had left the rose and the note. But he could handle her. Landon knew Evergreen's sweet spot. Though they had never made love, Landon knew what ignited the fire in Evergreen. He had felt the heat of desire course through his veins, even before he had ever touched Evergreen. And the more she stood her ground and denied Landon an audience with her, the intensity of speaking with her, made Landon yearn for what he had never had.

Landon knew she was going to be madder than a wet hen. But, he could not leave the concert without at least speaking to Evergreen. In reality, he really did enjoy the concert. Evergreen had been blessed with the true talent of song. The realization had hit him in the barn one day. Evergreen had begged her mom and dad for guitar. That day she brought the guitar to the barn for Landon to see began the first step toward her journey of becoming a country music songwriter. Every opportunity, every chance, every minute she could play, Landon would become her audience. The bond of friendship had grown through the years, until they each knew what the other was thinking before they even said it. Evergreen could tell when Landon approved of a song. The smile in his eyes as she sang to him. Evergreen adored the fact that he genuinely cared to give his opinion.

As Evergreen looked at Landon, she could not help but candidly look at the man he had become. His blondish – brown hair was longer than when he had left her. He had parted it on the side. He was wearing a pink Henley long-sleeve shirt that showcased his arms. His jeans were tight in all the right places. And the best part was his boots. They were not new. She could tell. They were scuffed and worn. Landon was not a materialistic man. When it came right down to it, Landon Dawson radiated sensuality in the highest form. Many times in their barn stall, she would position herself to have her legs crossed over his. His hand would reach under Evergreen's long hair and pull her closer to his lips. Landon was Evergreen's first kiss. Evergreen remembered that he had pulled her head toward his. He had taken his thumb and stroked her bottom lip until it was swollen with desire. Oh yes, Landon Dawson knew exactly what he was doing and what he had done to Evergreen. She snapped out of the memory to look Landon square in the eyes. "Whatever you are going to say, save it. I don't care. I don't want to hear it."

There was no doubt in Landon's mind that he had not only hurt Evergreen emotionally, but he had literally pissed her off. Landon chuckled. "I was just going to tell you how incredible you and the band were, that the entertainment was top-notch, and ask how you are doing. But I can see how you are doing, Evergreen. You have a God-given talent, and I am so proud that you pursued your dream. You always talked about becoming a country music artist, and you did." Landon knew she was listening, because Evergreen had not backed away. This was his opportunity. What is the old saying? *Carpe diem* – seize the moment. Without analyzing why, he did.

He reached for her hand and pulled her close to him. He did not give her time to pull away. He placed his other hand under Evergreen's long, flowing blonde hair at the nape of her neck. And without hesitation, Landon Dawson kissed Evergreen Colt. It had been an eternity. Her lips parted to protest, but Landon had entwined his fingers with Evergreen's. A startled breath escaping from Evergreen's lips gave Landon the moment to deepen the kiss. Her lips were full of the sweetness that Landon needed. Her scent was that of the mist on the open sea. Landon knew when the kiss had turned into desire. Evergreen's body betrayed her and molded into his arms. Landon could not pull himself away. And then, the unthinkable occurred. Evergreen opened her lips to allow Landon access to heaven.

Evergreen's emotions were on high alert. She did not care to hear what Landon Dawson needed to say. His words were like butter, slick and smooth. She would not be caught off guard. She was about to turn to walk away from Landon when he grabbed her hand, and without any warning, pulled her close to him. His scent brought those memories flooding back. Musk. It was rich, sexy, and sensual, just as she recalled. Evergreen was in big trouble, and there was no escape. His other hand moved to the side of her neck and, then, cupped her long hair to have easier access to the side. His thumb was rubbing in circular motions from the bottom of her ear lobe to the slender part of her neck. A small shiver coursed through Evergreen's body. It was this instant that Evergreen knew she did not want Landon to stop. The realization that she did not want the kiss to stop brought Evergreen back to the moment at hand. She opened her eyes and saw Will walking towards them from a distance.

"Stop!" Evergreen placed both her hands on Landon's chest to capture his attention. *Okay,* she thought to herself, *that was not a good move.* Now, Landon was holding her hands tight to his chest. A chest that was muscular and brawny. She was in more than a little bit of trouble. "Landon, let go. I need to go meet Will. My manager. He's headed this way."

Landon released Evergreen's hands, but not without noticing that Evergreen was …oh, what was that old saying his mother would tell him when she caught Landon in a lie? Oh yeah: "as nervous as a cat in a room full of rocking chairs".

CHAPTER 8

Evergreen stepped back and waved her hand to motion Will to where she was with Landon. As Will approached, Landon had an uneasy feeling that he was not going to like Evergreen's manager. Will drew closer and then, without pausing, kissed Evergreen on the lips that Landon had just kissed. Yep, he did not like Will.

Landon looked at Evergreen, who was blushing. "Evergreen, are you going to introduce me to your manager?" Evergreen could tell that Landon had surmised that Will was not *just* her manager. There was something more to their relationship than client / manager. The awkward silence that ensued gave Landon the information that he recognized. Evergreen turned back to Landon and began with, "Landon, this is Will, mine and the band's manager." Will looked a bit perplexed. Landon extended his hand towards Will.

"And you are….?" Will inquired. Landon could tell that question had Evergreen squirming. Evergreen had a look of trepidation waiting to hear Landon's reply. Landon wanted to knock Evergreen's boots off, but knew at this moment if he said what he was thinking, it would only do more damage. "I am a friend of Evergreen's. A very close friend. We grew up together. I had no idea that EC and the Daybreak Band was Evergreen Colt," Landon stated. Will did not return the smile. He swung his attention back to Evergreen and asked her to follow him back to where the band was going over the next day's schedule. Evergreen told him she would be there in just a minute and not to start the meeting without her. Will leaned in and kissed Evergreen's cheek. Will looked at Landon and returned to where the band had seated themselves on a picnic table, near the bus.

In less than five minutes—that's all the discussion lasted—Landon knew he did not like Will. And from the looks of how Evergreen was staring at Landon, she knew it as well. Evergreen stepped back. "Landon, it was good to see you, but I need to get back to my band. We have a lot to go over before tomorrow. Maybe our paths will cross again."

What did she just say? Maybe their paths would cross again. Oh, they were going to cross. Not only were they going to cross, but Landon was pretty darn sure she would be on the same path he was taking. Landon could always tell when Evergreen became concerned or nervous about a situation. It was a dead giveaway. Landon walked with direct intention to Evergreen and positioned himself in Evergreen's way. He looked Evergreen in the eyes and said, "Stop fretting. Go check on the band and your manager. I will see you tomorrow."

"Not likely," Evergreen commented.

Landon squeezed her hands within his, "I will see you tomorrow, Evergreen. You can count on it."

As she began the walk towards the band and Will, Evergreen turned around. Well, that was a mistake. He was still there. He was still standing there. And he was still standing there staring at her. Never, ever did Evergreen believe she would see Landon again. Seeing him tonight had stirred the pot of emotions. Emotions she had kept hidden and concealed. In her travels with her band and with her manager, she had never mentioned the name of Landon Dawson.

CHAPTER 9

As she approached the band, Evergreen could see that the band members were talking with Gus, their bus driver. They were deep in discussion as she approached. The closer she got, she could hear the words "later", "may not be", "a week at the most". Evergreen knew what the next words were going to be. She cleared her throat to give them warning she was in the vicinity. All heads turned and looked at her. Gus stepped towards her.

"No, don't even tell me. I can already surmise from the look on everyone's face this is not going to be good news." Gus had been with the band for quite some time. Evergreen trusted him as their driver. Sometimes, Gus would be driving for the better part of a day. Evergreen knew that if Gus needed to pull over for a bit of rest, he would. But Gus always had her and the band at the venue at the appointed time—and usually, earlier than requested.

Gus looked at Evergreen. "Oh, sugar, do you want the good news or the bad news first?"

"Surprise me," Evergreen replied.

"Well, the good news is that we have the financial means necessary to pay for the repairs."

"And, the bad news?" Evergreen inquired.

"It's going to be a few days before we can get back on the road," Gus stated.

"How many days is 'a few days', Gus?" Evergreen asked.

"Three to four at the most is what the mechanic told me. They are on their way to come tow it to the shop. We made it here on a wing and a prayer. We cannot tempt fate and travel any further. It would be too dangerous," Gus told Evergreen.

Evergreen nodded her understanding of the predicament. The band and production crew would need a place to stay for the next few nights. As if her thoughts could be read by all, Will commented, "We need to get rooms for all of us while the bus is being repaired." All turned to look at Evergreen.

"Why are you guys looking at me? I don't know anyone here. Fans, yes. Friends, no." Before she could even say it, she thought it. Yes, she did have a friend here. *Please, sweet Jesus, don't let me have to ask for his help after I just walked away from him.*

Will looked at her. "I think you do have at least one friend who may be able to help us."

Evergreen knew what she had to do. He was going to love the fact that she had to eat crow. Good lawd, she hated to ask him for help of any kind. Evergreen walked to the front of the stage to see if he was still part of the crowd that still lingered. Yep, he was still there. Joy of joys. *Well, here goes nothing*, she thought. Evergreen had a purpose to her walk. Evergreen could tell that Landon was with his friends. They were gathered in a tightknit circle, enjoying the evening. Even Landon was laughing. Evergreen smiled to herself. She missed his laugh. She did not want to intrude, but knew it was required. Evergreen told herself to suck it up. She knew Landon would help. He was a doctor. He was a pediatrician. It was just in his nature. It had been from the first day that Evergreen had met Landon. Plain and simple, he cared. *Sweet niblets*, courage had left her. Her legs stopped and did not move. At that moment, Landon's eyes locked with Evergreen's. Something was wrong.

CHAPTER 10

Landon saw her stop. It was as if she had hit a brick wall. Evergreen was looking at him. Her eyes were staring at Landon. He looked at his friends and informed them he would be right back. It took less than ten steps to reach her. When he did, Landon could see the small little tear that she was trying to hold back. He could tell. He knew it. Something had taken place. Again, Landon could only do what he knew to do. He held his hand out, hoping Evergreen would reach for him.

"Hey, I saw you coming towards the crowd. What's going on?" Landon calmly asked.

Evergreen was overwhelmed. She was tired from the long road trip. Even more, she needed to sit for more than five minutes. She was afraid her legs were going to buckle. *Lord, don't let me fall in front of him,* Evergreen thought.

"Landon, I need you," Evergreen began.

Before she could tell him why, Landon immediately responded "Tell me. How can I help?"

Evergreen could not stop the tear from trickling down. Worse, she could not stop the onslaught of the rest of the tears. It was as if they were like a waterfall. They just kept coming. She needed to wipe them away, but with what? He reached his hands forward and told her to shut her eyes. Landon gently swept the tears away from Evergreen's cheeks.

"Open your eyes, Evergreen and look at me. I am here. I will help. Tell me what is needed."

Everyone knows there's always a moment that changes the direction of your life. Why did Evergreen feel uncertain of the future? Two minutes ago, she knew the entire calendar for the rest of the year. Within a span of ten steps, her future seemed unsure.

Evergreen pulled her hands from Landon's. "We need hotel rooms for the night. The tour bus broke down before we arrived, and we barely made it here. It needs to be fixed and is going to require a few days in the repair shop to accomplish this. I did not know who else to ask. I apologize that I am coming to you, Landon, with all of my baggage, but I had nowhere else to go."

Landon laughed. "Is that it? You just need rooms to stay in? That's an easy fix. Come with me, and let's get the ball rolling." And just like that, Landon took her hand and led her to his group of friends, who were watching and wondering what in the world Landon was doing with country music star "EC" – Evergreen Colt.

"Don't worry. Trust me. Everyone is going to like you, and everyone will be happy to help." Landon squeezed Evergreen's hand for reassurance. The group divided, just like watching the Red Sea divide when Moses held his hands wide. Landon pulled Evergreen in front of him, so he could place his hands around her petite waist. This small gesture was to help Evergreen feel secure, but instead, the touch of his hands on her waist did not make her feel secure. Instead, it made Evergreen remember. His touch. His touch had always been gentle.

"Guys," Landon began, "I would like to introduce you to a close friend of mine, Evergreen Colt." Landon's friends could tell by the way Landon had pulled Evergreen into his chest that this was no close friend. Oh no. This was something more. Rikkie was the first to step forward. Landon knew she would be. Rikkie was the extrovert of the group.

"Hi, I'm Rikkie. I work with your 'close' friend at the children's hospital. How can we help?"

Landon whispered in Evergreen's ear, "See—I told you all would be well. Trust me."

Evergreen did trust him. She looked at Landon's friends and began with the first issue at hand. "The band and production crew need rooms to stay in for a few nights. Our bus broke down, and it needs to have repair work done before we can head to the next gig."

Before she could begin with any additional problems, Evergreen heard a voice speak from within the confines of the group. She could not see the young lady, but she heard her say, "My mom and dad own a bed and breakfast called The Dreamer Bed and Breakfast. It's a Victorian home here in town, and it can accommodate up to 25 guests. I'll call Dad and let him know we are on our way over. If the band and production crew do not mind, it's within walking distance. Everyone can grab their luggage, and we can head out. My parents are going to love the fact that we will be busy."

Landon looked at Evergreen and said, "And that was none other than Miss Teegan Wright. Her nickname is 'TeeTee'. She has a heart of gold. So, are we set?" Landon looked at Evergreen, waiting for an answer.

Evergreen did not know whether to cry or to kiss him. She was so grateful for what had just transpired in less than 15 minutes. Either way, Evergreen was elated to tell Gus, the band, and the crew that they would have a place to sleep for the next few nights. Without thinking, she turned into Landon's chest and threw her arms around his neck and kissed the side of his cheek. "I can never repay you, Landon, for your kindness. I'll run back and tell the boys what the plan is and return."

Evergreen had caught Landon off guard. He did not expect the kiss. Nor did he expect the way his body was reacting. Landon smiled. "I can never repay you" were the words. Oh yes. There was a way for Evergreen to repay him. Not at this particular moment, but there would be a time when the favor would be called in. Evergreen Colt could count on that.

CHAPTER 11

Landon watched as Evergreen began informing the band and production crew of what was to take place with lodging accommodations. All began bringing their luggage off the bus and walking towards Landon. He noticed that Evergreen was speaking to Will, "the manager". Will was clasping Evergreen's hand. They were headed his way. As they approached closer to Landon and his friends, Landon saw Evergreen let go of Will's hand. She placed her hand on Will's chest. She was speaking about something, but Landon could not hear what. Evergreen was walking back. Landon did not know where, but he was going to find out.

Everyone was standing in a circle with luggage in hand. Tee Tee was beaming from ear to ear. Landon knew she was in her element. Tee Tee loved to plan special events. Oh, yes, the band and production crew were in for a treat. Tee Tee smiled and raised her hands in the air to get everyone's attention.

"Guys, we are less than a block from my mom and dad's bed and breakfast. If you have everything, I'll lead the way." Just like that. This had been too simple. Way too easy. Landon did not have time to tell his friends that he was going to veer back towards the bus to check on Evergreen.

He knew that all were in capable hands. He also realized that listening to the group as they were leaving, there was excitement in the air for continuing the night at The Dreamer Bed and Breakfast. Oh, yes, southern hospitality was on overload. The band and production crew were going to be engulfed by southern hospitality. Landon took one look back before he began the walk towards Evergreen.

Evergreen told Will that she had forgotten something important. She had left it in her safe spot on the bus. She needed to retrieve it, to be sure it was put back in its rightful spot: in the back of her jeans pocket. Evergreen had never told anyone what was in the pocket. She opened the doors to the tour bus. She had informed Will it would only take a few minutes. She opened the bus doors and headed to the table where she would write music while on tour. No one knew, but the seat that Evergreen would sit on and write music raised up. A secret compartment only she knew about. Evergreen knew this was the place to keep documents and special things safe. She raised the seat up. It was there. Just as she had left it. She picked it up and placed it in the back pocket of her jeans.

She was walking to the front of the bus to catch up with the rest of the band when she heard a noise. The bus doors had opened. Who or what was coming through the doors? Evergreen's heart began to race. What should she do.? It was just her on the bus. There was no one else. She ducked down and slid behind the seat, so as not to be seen. Then, she heard, "Evergreen, Evergreen are you on here?" Evergreen was going to throttle him. What in the world was he doing?

"Landon Dawson, I am right here. You scared me half to death. Don't ever do that again."

As Evergreen turned to exit the bus, Landon was right there. She didn't just bump into him; she fell into him. She fell into a rock hard, very fit, masculine man. Before she could step back to catch herself, Landon had caught her and pulled her close within the confines of his sinewy arms. Evergreen knew she had just entered dangerous territory. She inhaled his scent. Oh yes, this brought back memories.

Landon stared into Evergreen's eyes. "I will never let you fall, Evergreen. I will always be there." Landon made that statement with such conviction that Evergreen allowed the wall to lower. The wall just didn't lower, Evergreen admitted to herself as she was standing tightly wrapped in Landon's embrace, the wall had crumbled.

"Look at me," Landon commanded. Evergreen knew deep within that if she did, it was over. For so long, she had never whispered his name. As of right now, the band and production crew still had no idea the relationship between Landon and his help he offered. All they knew was that Landon Dawson happened to be in the right place at the right time and was able to offer his assistance. Landon took his hand under Evergreen's chin and lifted it towards his lips.

CHAPTER 12

No, he could not kiss her. He had left her. She would not allow it. But her lips betrayed her, and, then, her body inched closer to Landon's. Landon took his finger underneath the small golden, velvet strap of Evergreen's cami and lifted it off her shoulders. He slid the strap down and leaned in to kiss her bare shoulder. A shiver flowed down Evergreen's spine. And yet, Landon had not kissed her. His lips began to travel the silhouette of Evergreen's neck. At first, he placed light kisses, and, then, as Landon moved to her ear, the kiss became more of a suckle. The gentle caressing of his tongue around the tip of Evergreen's ear. Evergreen could not help but move her head to the side, so Landon could play havoc on her senses of touch. As Landon moved closer to Evergreen's swollen lips, he knew she desired him. He had felt Evergreen's reaction to just touching him. Evergreen was his. She always had been. The only issue at hand was when. *When* would she be his?

Before Landon could think of any other questions, he found the corner of Evergreen's lip. He nibbled at first. Light, small kisses. Evergreen tried to turn her head.

"Don't", Landon told her. "Don't turn away from me. Let me taste all of you."

Evergreen shook her head no. This could not happen. It should not happen. Evergreen needed to tell Landon they would be noticed if they did not arrive at the bed and breakfast, but those words never left her. Instead, the kiss grew deeper, and soon, Landon's tongue was swirling around Evergreen's.

Evergreen felt as if she were floating. She never wanted to come down to earth. She wanted this feeling forever. It had been a long time since Evergreen's heart beat as fast as it was beating now, and it was all due to him. He had wreaked havoc on her life when he left her, and he was wreaking havoc on her life now that he had found her. Before she knew it, her hands had reached around Landon's neck and were playing with his hair. This was all the permission Landon needed. Evergreen was not leaving the embrace of his arms or the tour bus.

Landon deepened the kiss. He knew that Evergreen was feeling the effect of the kiss. She lay her head back in the palm of his hand. He slipped the other strap of the cami off her shoulder. Her shoulders were bare to Landon's touch. He could see the tips of her breasts rise and fall. Landon needed Evergreen. Every part of his body was reacting. He knew that Evergreen felt him. He took her hand and placed it on his manhood. If there was any doubt about how Landon felt about Evergreen, he could not deny it.

Evergreen did not know what to do or how to react. There had only been two relationships since she had been on the road as a country music artist. One was standing in front of her. The second was Will. Evergreen had never experienced the desire to know more about a man than she did right now. She began to massage Landon. Landon let out an expletive. This was torture. What was she doing? Did she know what she was doing to him?

Landon pulled her closer, so he could taste the swell of her breasts. He placed light kisses on the curvature of each breast. Evergreen did not know when her cami had fallen to her waist. Landon drew her nipple to a taut erection. His fingers were gentle. Evergreen was frozen. Her legs could not move. Evergreen was falling to pieces. This was not real. This was a dream.

"Open your eyes, Evergreen", Landon stated. "Open your eyes, so you can see the desire in mine." Evergreen did as Landon requested.

Big mistake. Huge mistake. Landon's eyes locked with Evergreen's. "Evergreen, tell me what you are thinking?"

Evergreen could not. If she told Landon her exact thoughts, not only would she be blushing, Evergreen was pretty sure she could make Landon's cheeks turn a pink tinge. "I can't, Landon," Evergreen whispered.

Landon pulled her closer to where he could bury his lips within the delicate curve of Evergreen's neck. "You *can* tell me, and you *will* tell me," Landon murmured. A shiver went down Evergreen's entire body. Landon felt it. He knew she wanted him. Why was she denying what was inevitable?

Evergreen attempted to pull away. "Landon, we need to return to the bed and breakfast. They will miss us. Trust me." Evergreen stated as a matter of fact. Landon chuckled. "I seriously doubt they will, Evergreen. They are preoccupied with check in and getting a good night's rest. Before she could even respond, Landon pulled Evergreen within his embrace. "You have nowhere to run, nowhere to hide, Evergreen. I cannot let you go. You are mine. I'm going to kiss you into tomorrow and all the days that God gives me."

Evergreen realized at that moment on her tour bus, she was exactly where she need to be: wrapped in Landon's embrace. Landon leaned in and tugged at Evergreen's swollen bottom lip.

"Open your lips for me, Evergreen. I want to know every inch of you." Evergreen was about to object when her lips betrayed her, and they opened to receive Landon's tongue. As Landon explored Evergreen's lips with quick nibbles, Evergreen could not breathe. She took a deep breath in. That was all Landon Dawson needed. Evergreen would not be leaving this bus. Landon would not make the same mistake twice.

Landon guided Evergreen's petite form to the sofa sleeper. He picked Evergreen up, all the while still kissing her. With movements as light as a feather, he lay Evergreen down. He placed both hands on each side of her face to steady himself and not to hurt Evergreen. Landon took his finger and trailed it down the center of her breastbone to her belly button, and to the top of her jeans. Landon had easy access to place his finger inside the ribbing of the jeans and feel Evergreen's reaction. With one hand, he had Evergreen's belt unbuckled and the button undone. The zipper slid down with ease.

To Landon's surprise, Evergreen was not wearing panties. She was bare to his touch. He smiled. Evergreen had never been conventional. He slid his hand around to cup her naked bottom. Evergreen bit her bottom lip. This was not how she had pictured the concert ending. This was not how she imagined the evening. But oh, it felt so right. There was no place else she needed to be at this moment in time. Evergreen was where she had always dreamed. She was in Landon's arms. She looked at Landon, who was staring at Evergreen as if this was the first time he had ever seen her. Evergreen placed her hand on the side of Landon's face. "Landon, what's wrong? Are you okay?"

What was wrong? she had asked him. Nothing. Nothing was wrong. Everything was right. Everything was as it should be. For the first time he could remember, Landon knew exactly where he was supposed to be and who he was supposed to be with: this exquisite lady who was laying unadorned in his arms. She had no idea that she held all the cards. Landon had been captured.

"Evergreen, nothing is wrong. There is no more perfect moment than this." Landon leaned in and kissed her on her forehead. He then travelled to each eye. He kissed each side of her cheek with such gentleness. Landon tugged at the bottom of her ear lobe with his lips and softly spoke into her, "You are not leaving tonight, Evergreen. I am not letting you go. I cannot let you go."

Evergreen could not speak. She nodded her head. Landon pulled her to a standing position and removed her blue jeans. He stopped on the way down. He chuckled. Those cowboy boots were a bit of a problem. He looked into Evergreen's eyes and said, "We can make love with the boots on or off. Your choice." Evergreen sat down, and Landon removed the boots. His movements were slow and intentional. When the last boot was removed, Landon slid the jeans down the rest of the way. That was more like it. She was a vision to Landon.

Evergreen did not know if she was breathing or not. She could not move. She was frozen in time. Her body was betraying her. It was reacting to every whisper, kiss, and touch of Landon. Evergreen could not deny it to Landon, nor to herself.

Landon began to unbuckle his pants. She reached out to help him. Landon inhaled. She could sense the change in her and in Landon. She stood up. Evergreen began to tug Landon's shirt from his blue jeans. With purpose, she took her time, placing a kiss as the shirt would rise higher. When she had reached as high as her petite frame could lift, Landon help take the shirt off.

"Evergreen, come here." The kiss was tender and soft. Landon felt Evergreen's mouth open for his tongue to taste what he had desired for so long. Evergreen could not prevent her arms from wrapping around Landon's neck. Landon did not have the will to stop. Evergreen moaned his name. That was all Landon needed. He lay Evergreen on the couch. He felt her wrap her legs around his. "Careful, Evergreen, you're playing with fire."

Evergreen shook her head. "I know what I'm playing with: it's you," and she reached for Landon's manhood, which was swollen with desire.

Landon did not know how much longer he could maintain self-control. He took his hand and trailed it slowly, like ice melting down Evergreen's belly. He stopped to place a kiss on her bellybutton. He felt Evergreen take a breath in. His mouth followed the line of his kisses. Landon's hand went to the inside of Evergreen's leg. She shifted her leg. Landon slid his finger down the inner side of Evergreen's leg and then touched Evergreen's most inner being. Landon watched Evergreen. Her eyes closed and her lips slightly parted. Her back arched to meet the strokes of Landon's. He moved his body to accommodate Evergreen's petite frame. He was now facing Evergreen. He stimulated the tip of her clitoris with his manhood.

"Evergreen, look at me," Landon commanded. Evergreen opened her eyes. She knew what she had dreamed was going to happen. She could not turn back. She did not want to turn back. "Evergreen," Landon said, "now is the time to tell me to stop."

Evergreen shook her head. She did not want Landon to stop. Her body was yearning for that moment. "No, Landon, I do not want to stop. I have never been surer of anything. Please."

"Please what, Evergreen?

"Please take me." Evergreen positioned her hands on Landon's derrière. Landon began to tease Evergreen's vagina with the tip of his manhood.

In and out in a slow, rhythmic movement, Landon desired to bring her to heights of euphoria. Landon did not know how much longer he could maintain his willpower not to ravish Evergreen. Landon gazed upon her. He did not know how he could be so blessed. He wanted everything to be just right. Landon felt a change in Evergreen's response. Evergreen was guiding Landon to heaven. He slowly entered where he knew ecstasy awaited.

Evergreen softly spoke his name. "Landon, I need you. I need to feel you inside." Landon began slow, thrusting movements. He wanted to be sure that he did not hurt Evergreen. To his surprise, Landon did not have to worry about that. Evergreen pulled Landon inside of her. Evergreen was warm as he waited for her to adjust to his entry. She was tight.

There was no way that Landon could reveal to Evergreen that she was the one who could send his heart into a frenzied bliss with just a kiss. Release was needed. Landon did not know how much longer he could hold to restrain. Evergreen's body echoed the desire on her face. She smiled up at Landon. Hot fires ignited Willow's desire. The fires of passion mirrored on Landon's face.

"Landon, please," Evergreen begged.

"Tell me again, Evergreen. Tell me what you want?"

"You, Landon Dawson, I want all of you," Evergreen told him.

"I am yours, and I have always been yours," Landon told her.

With that confession, Evergreen said, "Then take me. Take me to where I will never return." This what Landon had waited to hear. He could not help himself when he thrust into the most sacred area of Evergreen. Landon was falling and could not stop. He gave Evergreen time for her body to adjust to what had happened. With small strokes in and out, Landon found pleasure in Evergreen's moans of satisfaction. His movements became intense and focused.

Evergreen was floating. She was floating higher than the clouds on a warm, sunny day. This was not happening. There was nothing that could describe the emotions that were racing through her mind or affecting how her body was reacting to Landon. There was something that had been missing. That something was Landon. Even now, she did not want to admit what her mind had already accepted. Sometimes, the most beautiful things in love cannot be heard or seen, only felt from within. Evergreen knew that every moment moving forward would be the most precious.

Landon felt the change in Evergreen. Landon's lips covered Evergreen's lips in a long, warm kiss that took her breath away. He deepened his thrusts and felt the moistness of Evergreen's instinctive response. She arched her back to feel Landon deepen himself inside of her. His reaction was that of necessity. Evergreen knew when Landon was ready to release. Landon pulled her closer to him in a sitting position.

Evergreen was going nowhere. She was where she needed to be, in his arms. He positioned Evergreen on top of his manhood and lowered her down. Landon no longer had control over his body. The release of satisfaction plunged through his body. This was heaven. This was his Evergreen. He felt her body tighten around him, and knew when she experienced heaven, as well.

Evergreen did not know what had overcome her. She placed her head on Landon's shoulders. She did not want to move from the warmth that was surrounding her. She whispered in Landon's ear, "Please tell me it will always be like this."

Landon smiled. Did her statement mean what he thought it meant? She was already thinking of the next time they would make love? Landon shifted a bit to accommodate her petite body. "Evergreen, I promise you, it will not only be like this, it only gets better."

She mumbled, "Good, I was afraid it would not." Landon chuckled. He knew she was falling into a deep sleep from their lovemaking. He knew they would not make it back to the bed and breakfast.

Landon could accommodate both their bodies on the small makeshift sleeper on the bus. He maneuvered himself so that Evergreen was scooped into his body. He remembered the term one of his friends had used: "spooning". This was the only way. Landon did not mind that he would need to hold Evergreen as she slept. At the end of the sleeper, he saw a blanket. He could only surmise it was Evergreen's. He grabbed it without waking Evergreen and spread the blanket over both of them. He laughed to himself. He had forgotten how tiny Evergreen was. There was no blanket to cover his entire body. His knees and feet were left uncovered. It did not matter. This night. This woman. He loved Evergreen Colt. With that last thought, Landon drifted to sleep with no thought of the morning.

CHAPTER 13

Evergreen could not move. Was she dreaming? What in the world was going on? Why could she not move? Her eyes were still heavy. She was warm. She was holding on to the edge of her favorite blanket. Before she could realize what was taking place, she heard his voice against her ear, "Evergreen, if you keep moving and shifting your body, I'm going to straight up tell you, you're going to be very upset with me," Landon chuckled. Evergreen punched him in the stomach with her elbow.

Before Landon could appropriately respond to that little punch, both felt a bump. Evergreen panicked. Landon's eyes were pretty wide.

"Landon Dawson, you need to get up now and move like lightning," Evergreen pleaded. Landon could not help but laugh. "Evergreen, honey, why the hurry?" Then, there was another bump, which bounced Evergreen right on the floor. Landon started laughing and could not stop.

"Landon, we are moving. The bus is moving," Evergreen stated with panic in her voice.

Landon pushed the curtain to the side. Sure enough, the tour bus was moving.

"I need to get dressed." Evergreen looked at him. "You need to get dressed, too. We need to figure out what in the world is going on." Both began the search for their clothes. Trying to remember where everything had been thrown from the night of lovemaking was making the ordeal more time-consuming.

The tour bus came to a halting stop, which threw Evergreen into Landon's bare chest. She took a deep breath in. This morning was not going as she had planned. The entire concert, if she were honest, was not the typical concert she had become accustomed to playing. Landon was holding her and watching her. What was that pretty little mind thinking?

Before he could ask her, both Landon and Evergreen heard a voice. "Tires need to be looked at. Might as well go ahead and do an oil change and rotate the tires since we are here." Evergreen knew that voice. It was Gus, her driver.

The next voice they heard replied, "It should only take a couple of days to do everything on your list. Will this suffice?" Okay, that was not a voice Evergreen recognized. She looked at Landon with an inquiring eyebrow and, then, it hit Landon. They were at Peyton's Gas Station. This was the family-owned gas station – repair shop that most of the town patronized. "It's okay, Evergreen. We are at Peyton's Gas Station. I know the family," Landon stated with confidence.

"That's just peachy", Evergreen started. "What are we going to do? How are we going to…" and then, the tour bus doors opened.

Evergreen turned her head to where she knew Gus would be standing. "Well, well, good morning, Miss Evergreen. How are you doing? Do you need anything? Would you like to introduce me to…" Gus pointed straight at Landon. Gus could not wait to hear the explanation on this finding. Both looked pretty guilty from where Gus was standing.

As soon as Landon heard the gentleman call Evergreen "Miss Evergreen", Landon immediately liked him. Gus reminded him of a more mature version of Willow and Landon's father. Landon stretched his hand towards Gus. "Please excuse Miss Evergreen. The morning has taken a different path than what was anticipated. She's a bit out of sorts. My name is Landon Dawson. I am a dear friend of Miss Evergreen's." Gus liked Landon. He had a sense of humor. I'm Gus. The tour bus driver and protector of Miss Evergreen.

Evergreen was in a pickle. She had never been in this predicament. As in most bands, privacy was kept between the band and her. No questions were asked regarding relationships. Many of the crew and band did not have a steady girlfriend or were even married. Life on the road, concerts, and travelling ten months out of the year was not for the faint at heart. Plain and simple, there was just no time for anything else.

Evergreen began to blush. Could Gus see the change? Gus looked at Evergreen before smiling and stating, "Can't wait to hear how you and Mr. Dawson ended up on the bus."

Landon smiled and interrupted Gus with a pat on his back. "Actually, it's Dr. Dawson, and believe you me, I cannot wait to hear the story, as well. It's gonna be, what's the term, Evergreen, that you used with me when we were growing up? Oh yes, a wing dinger of a story."

CHAPTER 14

A doctor. Landon a doctor. She remembered that growing up he had always wanted to be a pediatrician. She had never thought to ask him about his career. And now, the cat was out of the bag. Landon saw Evergreen's eyes raise in surprise.

He leaned closer to Evergreen. "Caught you off guard, did I?"

Evergreen did not know what to say. And now this, where should she start the story with Gus? How much should she tell him, and how much could he surmise what had taken place?

Gus laughed. "It's okay. All will be well. Let's get you and Dr. Dawson off the bus. I need to finalize the rest of the paperwork for the repairs on the bus. We can walk back to the bed and breakfast. That way, you can clear your head and you can tell me the story of how you and Dr. Dawson ended up on your tour bus well into the night and the morning."

Evergreen hugged Gus. He looked at her and chuckled. Gus could always make Evergreen feel safe. He was always giving sound advice. Gus had been on the road most of his life with one or two bands. Evergreen had found Gus when he had been in between jobs. He had been a Godsend. Evergreen knew that Gus would never steer her wrong. He always had advice, but more importantly, he always had words of encouragement when Evergreen came up against her biggest obstacle: herself.

Evergreen watched as Gus discussed what was needed in repairs. He signed the paperwork, shook the attendant's hand, and walked out with a smile. He looked right at Evergreen and grinned with big ole smile. Evergreen knew it was coming. She could not lie to Gus. Evergreen was mentally preparing herself. As she was walking towards the bed and breakfast, she turned to see Landon and Gus standing beside each other, watching her. She placed her hands on her hips. "What? What have I done now?"

Landon could not help it. He knew she was not headed in the right direction, but he was not about to tell her. He was perfectly content watching Evergreen walk. She had a cute butt. Landon was taking notice of several things about Evergreen. She was on a mission. Each step was made with purpose. Landon winked at Gus and said, "How long do you want to give her until we tell her?"

Gus chuckled. "I'm not getting her shorts in knot. You go right ahead, Dr. Dawson."

"Call me Landon, please, Gus."

When Evergreen turned around, Landon knew the gig was up. Evergreen knew they had been speaking about her. When she put her hands on her hips, she meant business. Evergreen had only done that when she was tired and frustrated. From the looks of the stare she was giving Landon and Gus, she was both at the moment.

"Evergreen, sweetheart, you're going in the wrong direction. The bed and breakfast is this way. Come on. We are not that far." Gus watched as she stomped back.

"Fine, show me the way, Dr. Dawson." Now, Landon knew she was really ticked.

Before Landon could steer her in the right direction, Gus interrupted with, "How about we grab some grub. To be honest with both of you, I am starvin' marvin." Evergreen did not want to admit it, but her tummy had been growling. She could use the boost to get the morning started.

"Landon, what's the best restaurant in town for breakfast?" Landon knew of several hotspots, but the one he loved was Colonel Hawk's Place. It was the best southern cookin' around.

"If you feel like walking and enjoying the morning, we are not far from a wonderful venue."

Gus looked at Evergreen. Evergreen looked at Gus. Both smiled and said, "Why not?"

Landon loved his hometown. He loved working at the children's hospital. He loved his co-workers, but more, he loved the country atmosphere that Hopeulikit offered to all who had taken up residence and even the tourists.

The morning was warm, and the sun was rising. Evergreen loved to feel the sun on her face. It had been too long since she had been back home. She missed the farm. She missed her parents even more. Landon was watching Evergreen from the corner of his eye. Last night had been nothing but short of spectacular. Did she feel the same way? Neither had time to ask each other. Evergreen felt his stare. Landon was saying something, but all she could focus on were his lips. *Shake it off*, she told herself. *Get a grip.*

Landon was informing them the venue was just around the corner. She smiled at Landon and winked. Now why she did that was beyond her. Evergreen felt as if she were on top of the world. She could not keep herself from smiling. She was happy in the moment. She threw caution to the wind with that wink. Evergreen would tackle that dilemma later. For now, she was with the two most handsome guys in the universe.

"There it is," Landon stated. "Colonel Hawk's Restaurant." Landon looked at both Gus and Evergreen. "You are both in for a treat," I promise.

As they approached, Evergreen had no idea what to expect, but it was not this. There was a line outside to get in. Tables that were already filled were set up along the sidewalk. Evergreen noticed that folks were staring at her. They were more than likely trying to figure out if she was EC, the country music artist, from the night before. She smiled at each one and said, "Good morning."

The door opened. Evergreen knew that smell. That was the frying of bacon and waffles being made. Oh, and that syrup smell. Evergreen thought to herself, please have fried taters and ripened red tomatoes. Better yet, what if they had fried bologna? Landon watched Evergreen. He knew he had chosen the right spot. Even Gus was nodding his approval.

Walking in, Landon said, "If we eat at the bar, we can watch the head cook, and the smell is ten times better."

Evergreen took his hand and entwined hers. "Thank you, Landon. This is exactly what I needed."

Landon looked at Evergreen and said, "I know".

Gus commented, "This is just what the doctor ordered."

They sat down, and their server, Neesie, greeted them with a "Hello sugar, what can I get you folks this morning?"

Oh yes, this is what Evergreen needed and had missed the most – southern manners. Neesie took their orders and told them it would be about 10 to 15 minutes, and that breakfast would be served piping hot. Landon had made sure that Evergreen sat in the middle of him and Gus.

He leaned his head forward and said, "What happens after breakfast? Is there any place special you need to be?"

Evergreen looked at Gus and asked, "Do we have to be any place special?"

Gus laughed and said, "Well, if we did, it's too late now. Whatcha got in mind, Doc?" That's what Landon wanted to hear. He would have Evergreen with him for a few more hours.

"I would like to take you to Lullaby Children's Hospital and give you the ten-cent tour, so to speak."

They finished breakfast. Evergreen watched as Neesie came from behind the cash register and hugged Landon. "It was good to see you, Doc," she said. Neesie looked at Evergreen and Gus and hugged them. "Don't be a stranger. And if ya have time, come on back for supper." Evergreen had never felt such euphoria as she did right now.

CHAPTER 15

Landon looped his finger inside Evergreen's belt buckle, which meant the rest of his hand was on her hip. A shiver went up Evergreen. She knew she was not cold, but that one small gesture had an effect on her entire body. Evergreen watched as Landon leaned in to kiss Neesie on the side of her cheek and thank her again. Neesie blushed. He had not changed. Landon was still a charmer. He nodded to Gus in the direction of the door. Just like that, the morning was half over.

Evergreen could not explain the feeling in the pit of her stomach. She was nervous and excited at the same time. Landon had invited her into his world. What was his world? What were his days like as a pediatrician? Evergreen did not realize they had stopped walking. Landon had noticed that Evergreen was thinking. He knew she was thinking, because she had been pulling on her earlobe. The only time Evergreen did this was when, as his grandma would say, "folks are fretting over something". If she kept tugging on that earlobe, she was going to rub it raw. He positioned himself in front of Evergreen, so she would stop right in front of his chest. She looked up.

"What, what's going on?"

"You didn't notice that Gus went back to the bed and breakfast. You've been lost in your own thoughts. I didn't want to interrupt you. It's just you and me," Landon informed her.

Evergreen turned around. Yep, Gus was gone. She was alone with Landon again. They were already standing at the entrance. Evergreen looked up to see the name. She loved it. Lullaby Children's Hospital.

Landon reached for both her hands. "Don't be nervous. Trust me, okay?" Evergreen nodded.

They walked in, and, immediately, the smell of cotton candy hit her senses. The first-floor décor consisted of rocking chairs and cradles, and written on the walls were the rhymes and poems that children could easily memorize. Placed by each rocking chair was a small table with either a puzzle or coloring book and crayons.

Evergreen inquired, "And what about the germs from little hands?"

Landon smiled. "They are free for each child who walks in that door. And as soon as a child takes one, they are replaced with a new one. All are sanitized before being placed on the table. And, if you turn your pretty head around, you will see the Grammie of the hospital at the info desk. This is her area. We don't mess with Grammie," Landon winked at Grammie. "She keeps the staff in line, and she loves the children as if they were her own."

Landon kept walking. Evergreen had forgotten how long his legs were, and he was on a mission: nothing could stop him, not even her short legs.

"The elevator is over this way. We just need to go to the third floor. That's my floor."

"Sounding pretty possessive, aren't we?" Evergreen commented. As the elevator doors closed, Landon grabbed Evergreen by surprise, pulled her close, and kissed her. Evergreen could not protest. Her lips betrayed her. They opened to allow entry for Landon's tongue. She felt the passion of Landon's need. She felt really hot. Was it her? Was she getting sick? He drew back and studied her face with hungry eyes.

The doors opened. Landon touched the side of her face and said, "We will continue this later."

As they walked off the elevator, the nurses said good morning to both of them. Landon introduced Evergreen as a dear childhood friend. Rikkie screamed, "I know you. You're EC, the country music singer we saw at the festival last night."

Evergreen nodded, "I am." Well, that opened up the can of worms. All of the nurses, and even a few of the doctors, made an appearance at the nurse's station. Landon had stepped to the side to watch as Evergreen—his Evergreen—answered all the questions the staff were throwing at her. Several had grabbed note paper to ask if she would personally autograph and write a message for a family member. And, then, the cell phones came out, and chaos ensued as to how many selfies and pics could be taken. Evergreen couldn't find Landon and for a brief moment, panic set in.

Landon had been observing how Evergreen was able to handle all the requests. He heard her answer each question that was asked about her career, and, then, he heard what every doctor hates to hear. "Are you okay?" he overheard Rikkie's voice.

Is who okay, he thought. In the pit of his stomach, he knew it was Evergreen. She was surrounded by so many. Growing up, Evergreen had told him she had feared only two things. She could not swim – so drowning was on the top of the list—but more so, Evergreen was claustrophobic. She could not stand to be enclosed with no way of exiting.

"Evergreen," he hollered over the nurses and doctors, "I'm here. I'm right here."

Evergreen fell into Landon's muscular chest. Landon turned around to see his mentor, Crispin Steele. I need to get her to a room, so she can rest," he whispered to Dr. Steele, praying he could read his lips.

Dr. Steele nodded. He knew that privacy was needed. Landon scooped Evergreen up in his arms and told her all was going to be okay. Landon looked down and knew she was close to her breaking point. A small tear had trickled down her cheek. He knew she did not want the staff to see her so vulnerable.

"I got you, I am not going to let you go," Landon spoke to her in a hushed tone. Dr. Steele opened the door to the empty room. It was a room that all little girls loved – the walls were covered in crowns and princesses. Dr. Steele informed Landon the room was his for as long as needed. Landon thanked him. As Dr. Steele was leaving, Evergreen thanked him as well.

"Don't mention it. Sometimes, we just need a few minutes to drop back fifteen yards and punt. Take your time." Dr. Steele told both Evergreen and Landon. Landon chuckled. He knew Evergreen had no idea what that analogy was, but she played it off very well.

CHAPTER 16

The door closed. Landon sternly told her to stay still. He was going to do a full examination to put his mind at ease.

Evergreen placed her hand in the air to stop him. "I'm okay. Really, I am," Evergreen assured him.

"I'll be the judge of that. Like I said, a full examination will be conducted, Miss Colt. I just need you to sit still and look pretty. Think you can do that for about fifteen minutes?", Landon inquired.

"Fine, fine, if it will make you happy, Dr. Dawson", Evergreen muttered under her breath. She did not think Landon had heard her rumblings. He placed his thumb underneath her chin. "I just need you to follow the doctor's orders. Not too difficult, is it?"

Evergreen did just as he told her. A thorough examination began. Evergreen had been on the road for a little over nine months without a break in concert dates. She did not know what had just happened, but she did not like it. She was still very lightheaded. Blood was drawn to get her white and red blood count. Blood pressure taken, and all the rest that goes along with being poked and prodded like a steer going to market. Landon had been gone for a few minutes. She knew that he was probably consulting with the nurse and the other technicians. She was very tired, and before she knew it, Evergreen had laid down on the hospital bed. She just needed a quick cat nap. She would only take 10 to 15 minutes, at the most.

Landon opened Evergreen's door to begin the tongue lashing, but upon seeing her sound asleep, he could not. He walked towards the bed and pulled another blanket out of the supplies. Rest. Plain and simple, rest was what was required. He turned the overhead light off and placed his hand on the side of her cheek. Evergreen mumbled something that he thought was, "You left me. Please don't leave me again." Landon quietly pulled his hand back and left the room.

Goodness, what time is it? Evergreen thought to herself. *Better yet, where am I, and how did I get here?* She raised herself up in the bed, and again, that feeling of the unknown set her emotions into play. She realized she was not in Kansas anymore, as the saying goes. Blinking several times to adjust her eyes to the room, she fathomed she was in a hospital bed. She could not breathe. She was sweating, and without thinking about the consequences, she screamed for Landon.

The door bolted open. "Hey, I'm right here. Everything's fine. Did you rest okay?" Landon questioned Evergreen.

"I think, so," Evergreen smiled.

"Good, your reports all came back normal. Evergreen, look at me. Tell me when the last time you had a good eight hours of solid sleep was," Landon questioned. Evergreen knew he did not want to hear the answer. Shoot a button, she did not want to tell him. Evergreen tried her best to play it off.

"What do you mean? I get sleep on the tour bus, Landon. I swear." Landon shook his head. Lawd, she was stubborn. She was going to skirt the question, the answer, and the entire issue. She had not changed one bit.

"Okay, let's try it another way – how many hours of uninterrupted sleep do you get, Evergreen?" Landon asked. Evergreen knew what was coming next. He was not going to like the answer. He was going to scold her and give her a lecture. He had not changed one bit.

"Landon, I get enough to do what needs to be done," Evergreen stated.

Landon was frustrated, and she could tell it. "Well, as a friend—a very dear friend and a pediatric doctor—I am going to let you in on a little secret: you suffered an anxiety attack. You have got to slow down and take care of yourself. Do I make myself clear? No more repeats of today. Let's get you back to the bed and breakfast, or Gus is going to think I kidnapped you."

Evergreen hated to admit that he was right. She needed to get back and check in with everyone. She did not want to reveal to Landon that the nap had done her good. Landon made her sign the patient hospital paperwork with suggested follow-up in two weeks, per Dr. Landon Dawson. She folded the paper up and went to place it in her back jeans pocket. Something was blocking the entry. Evergreen remembered. It was still there. She moved the instructions to the other side.

Landon was waiting outside her hospital room door. All business had resumed to normal. There was not a large group gathered at the nurses' station anymore. Instead, Evergreen saw Dr. Steele approach Landon and inquire if everything was fine. She saw Landon nod and smile and turn towards her. Dr. Steele patted Landon on his shoulder.

Landon was walking towards her. "Ready to head back?" he asked. Evergreen nodded "yes." When they had reached the first floor of the elevators, Landon said, "We are taking my vehicle. No more walking for you. I think you need to be chauffeured for all our sakes and peace of mind."

Evergreen chuckled. "Any other time, I would argue with you, but today, I will let you think you are right."

Landon's eyebrows shot up in the air. "Oh, Evergreen, I'm always right." Before she could reply, Landon drew her into his arms and kissed her lips with passion and intent. "Always mine," his voice turned into a whisper.

Landon guided Evergreen off the elevator and towards his truck. Evergreen was shocked. Being a doctor—and evidently a well-known pediatric doctor—she thought Landon would have something like a Mercedes-Benz or an Escalade, but no, it was the old truck that Landon's dad had purchased for him. Landon knew how to drive all vehicles on the farm before he could walk. She could not believe he had kept it, and more so, that it was still in good driving condition.

Landon opened the door for Evergreen to get in. "There have been a few adjustments to Ole Red, like seatbelts, but she's more or less what you remember."

Evergreen laughed. "You named her, Ole Red, Landon?"

"Of course, it's fitting—don't ya think?" Evergreen loved it. She had so many memories in this truck. So many good memories. "Wait til you hear her. She purrs like a kitten." Evergreen could not stop smiling. He was like a kid in a candy shop. There was such happiness in his eyes. "I'll get you back to the bed and breakfast in time for dinner. I doubt they will be serving breakfast." He reached to touch her hand. "Evergreen, are you okay?" She could hear in his voice the genuine concern.

Evergreen leaned over and kissed him on the side of the cheek. "Landon, I'm fine, really. Get me back before Ole Red turns into a pumpkin and the band sends out the search party."

"They pulled up to The Dreamer Bed and Breakfast. It looked as if half the town were sitting on the front porch. Evergreen saw Gus sitting on the steps. Landon parked, and Gus walked towards them. "Before you even get out, make sure both your stories are straight, or trust me, it ain't gonna be pretty with all the questions getting ready to fly at you."

Landon chuckled. He liked Gus. He could tell that Gus was protecting Evergreen and her reputation more than Landon's. "We do, Gus. All is good. And when we tell it, you won't believe it!"

Before Gus could say anything else, Evergreen's door had already been opened. All Landon heard was, "Where have you been?"

Gus flicked Landon on the shoulder. I have held off Will regarding questions of Evergreen's whereabouts. You're on your own.

Landon began to walk with Gus back to the porch. I got this, Landon smiled at Gus.

As a side note, Gus told Landon that Will had been managing the band and Evergreen for about three years now. Pretty darn good at managing and keeping us booked and on the road. The other side, I'm not too sure about." Landon knew what Gus was referencing.

Landon was exercising caution. He did not want Evergreen to know he was paying attention to Evergreen and Will. He thanked Gus for his kindness and told him he needed to be on his way. He needed to check to see if his little sister was still in town, or if she had already left to return to her home. He told Gus to explain to Evergreen why he had to leave. He asked Gus how much longer they anticipated being in town before the tour bus was fixed. Gus said the mechanics told him that it would only take one to two days, no later than Wednesday of the week. Landon nodded his head. He turned to walk back and saw Evergreen staring at him. As he opened the truck door and started the ignition, he saw Evergreen mouth the words "thank you." He smiled and backed out the driveway.

Driving back to his home, this was not how he had hoped the evening would end. For some reason, Landon was coming to the realization that he may never see Evergreen again. They each belonged to a different world. Would their worlds ever link to one another? As he pulled into the driveway, he could see Willow's car. She was still there. For some reason, that gave him comfort. He loved his sister. They argued with each other like most siblings, but when Landon was needing advice on the "female persuasion", Willow was there to break it down for him.

Landon not only needed "break it down" advice, but he wanted to question Willow as to his next move.

Willow heard the truck door slam, and knew Landon was home. She could not wait to hear his story of the last 48 hours. She knew something had taken place. The front door opened.

"Well, well, little brother, where have you been?"

Landon chuckled. "Always, straight and to the point. No pussyfooting around with you. Poor Dr. Bleu," Landon smiled. "Landon Dawson, don't give me that innocent look. It's too late. Spill the beans. What happened, and who with, and where did she go?"

"The concert was great. I had no idea it would be her on the stage. I thought my eyes were deceiving me. I did not know how successful she had become in the country music industry. When the band decided to go back to the bed and breakfast, I wanted to talk to her. I just did not know when the right moment would be until I saw her walk back towards her tour bus. As soon as I saw her, I kissed her. From that point, time stopped. We awoke to the bus moving. Getting dressed was quite hysterical. We were being towed. There was a knock on the door. It was their driver, Gus. The tour bus had been towed, and we were at the gas station. Gus, Evergreen, and myself went for a bite. Gus went back to the bed and breakfast. I took Evergreen to the hospital, so she could see where I worked. She passed out at the hospital. I took care of her. We left the hospital, and she's back at the bed and breakfast, and here I am," Landon stated as a matter of fact.

Willow looked at Landon. "I need to sit down. What about you? And what do you mean 'getting dressed was quite hysterical'? You were what....naked?"

Landon looked at Willow. "That's what you picked upon....that we didn't have clothes on."

"Absolutely," Willow laughed. "But I sense there's something amiss since you came home alone. Am I correct?"

There were times that Landon did not wish to share or speak to his little sister. and *this* was one of those times. "Willow, drop it. I don't want to talk about it. It's water under the bridge." Very seldom did Landon pull away from Willow when it regarded his relationships and girlfriends, but she knew that whenever SHE was mentioned, he went all solemn and quiet.

"I understand, Landon. I stayed to be sure you were okay. I need to get on the road. As my big brother, I try not to pry into your private life. I get it." Willow walked over to Landon and hugged him tight around the waist. "You've never let her go, have you?"

Landon shook his head. "Enough, Willow. Get on the road, and call or text when you get home, so I know you are okay."

CHAPTER 17

Will had approached Evergreen as soon as her feet hit the porch of the bed and breakfast. He embraced her in a bear hug, almost to the point she felt she was going to lose consciousness.

Evergreen laughed and pushed herself away from Will. "I wasn't gone that long, and besides, I was with Gus and the tour bus. We had to tow it to the mechanic's shop. You know how protective Gus can be. I'm fine." Evergreen stated. Will looked at her. He didn't believe her. He did a quick check from head to toe. She looked okay. And yes, the entire crew and band, and himself, trusted Gus with their lives—literally. Evergreen kissed him on the side of the cheek. "Let's go inside and make sure everyone else knows I'm okay." Evergreen did not feel like arguing nor giving any explanation of the last 36 hours. Evergreen turned one last time to see Landon leaving. As she entered the bed and breakfast, the door closed with a thud.

Landon was alone. Tomorrow was Monday, when he would return to work. Landon could only imagine the gossip that he knew had already taken place with Evergreen's quick visit. For the first time he could recall, he was not looking forward to work. It seemed like something had been left unfinished. He knew what it was. It was her.

Landon did not have her cell number. He only had the address of where the *entire* crew and band were staying. What the fudge nuggets (that's what Landon's mother would say when she felt the need to cuss)? What is going to happen if I do show up at the bed and breakfast? I could just say I was making a house call and checking on my patient. Lord, how corny did that sound? Even the thought of the word corny sounded old-fashioned. *Stop it, Landon. Just go to the bed and breakfast and see how she's doing. What are they going to do, ask you to leave?*

Landon showered and changed clothes. He was more comfortable in his jeans, boots, and Henley tees. He had thrown his hair up in a bun. Several of the nurses at the hospital had commented that they thought it was sexy when Landon placed it up in a bun. Maybe it was, maybe it wasn't, but for the most part, it was just easy. Last minute checks, and out the door he went. He had no idea what excuse he was going to give. No idea what he was going to say when he decided on the excuse. Landon was just going to pray, and pray unceasingly, as he recalled that one Bible verse.

Evergreen knew Will had a lot of questions. Before he could begin, though, Evergreen had told him when she walked through the door that she just needed to lay down for a bit. Will knew something was wrong. Evergreen never took a nap. Something had happened. What? He did not know, but he was bound and determined to get to the bottom of it. The band hollered for Evergreen to come sit with them on the back porch while they rehearsed a few songs for the next gig. Evergreen thought to herself that it might lift her spirits. She loved when she and the band could just sit around and play any song they wanted. Nothing was placed in stone as to a set of songs. Evergreen loved all the spiritual hymns she had grown up with. One of her favorites was "I'll Fly Away, Oh, Glory". There had been moments in Evergreen's life that she felt if she could just fly away, but being in the spotlight as a country music artist did not allow for those special moments.

As she and the band were finishing the song, she saw Will leave the opening of the back porch door. He must have heard something. Evergreen asked the band if they could remember the song "Standing in the Need of Prayer". All smiled. The band could not deny her request for any upbeat hymns. Just when she began to sing, she sensed more than saw, the something that Will had gone to check on was standing in the doorway to the back porch. She could tell Will was not happy.

He interrupted the band to inform them that Dr. Dawson had stopped by to check on his patient. Oh yeah, Will was in a mood. She was never going to be able to explain this where it all made sense. Shoot, it didn't even make sense to her.

Landon heard the music when he walked up to the bed and breakfast. He knocked several times. No one heard. He was about to turn the knob to walk in, when the door opened and revealed Will. "Can I help you, Dr. Dawson? Are you lost?" Will asked.

Okay, Landon knew when he heard sarcasm and facetiousness both at the same time. Landon knew that Will knew he lived here and was very familiar with the town and its amenities. "No, I just had a bit of time before I needed to prepare for tomorrow to return to work and wanted to follow up to see how Evergreen was feeling."

"And you couldn't have called to find out? You drove all the way over here? Wouldn't it have just been easier on both you and Evergreen if you had just picked the phone up?" Landon could recognize what was happening, and he didn't blame Will. Will was being protective of Evergreen. Maybe a bit overprotective. Landon hated to think he was going to have to become confrontational with Will to see Evergreen for himself.

Landon did not have to worry, because there stood Evergreen with both hands on her hips. She was not smiling – oh, no, that was *not* a smile. Her lips were pursed together, which reminded Landon of when they were younger. This only meant thing. She was going to have one of "those" discussions with him.

Evergreen looked at Will. "It's okay, sweetheart. I can handle Dr. Dawson and his concern for my well-being." With that statement, Will kissed her right smack dab on the lips. Evergreen thought the kiss would never end. She knew why Will had done this. She also knew Landon recognized this as well. Evergreen walked into the parlor area of the bed and breakfast.

"Are you guys serious?" Landon stated. Evergreen did not know if that was directed to her as a question, or just him making an offhand comment.

"I'm not sure, Landon. Since the first time I met Will, he has had my best interest and the band's best interest at heart. He has seen me through a lot of ups and downs. Whenever I needed someone's shoulder to cry on, he was there."

"Unlike me," Landon read between the lines.

"I did not say that," Evergreen walked towards him. She pointed her finger at his chest, "You did."

"Now, before the entire group that is sitting on the back porch comes in here curious as to what is taking place, please tell me you have something more than using my well-being to check up on me."

"Fine, I admit it. I wanted to see with my own eyes that you are okay. And just to be sure that you know I am serious, I brought my stethoscope with me to listen to your heart," Landon stated matter of factly.

"Let's get this over with then. I know you have to be at work in the morning bright-eyed and bushy-tailed for the kids, and Gus and I need to be at the station to check on the bus."

"Then come here, Evergreen Colt, so I can listen to the beats per minute of your heart." Well, if the fact that Landon wasn't standing right in front of her set it to beating, the fact that he used her entire name in a such a husky whisper did.

"Landon, can't you just look at me and tell that I am doing fine? It was just too much today with so many people around. You know how claustrophobic I get. I need an escape route, and I could not see one."

"So, what you just pass out, Evergreen? Nope, not buying it. One more time, please come here to me." That one statement of "come here to me" had set off alarms that Evergreen knew she should pay attention to, but Landon reached out his hand to Evergreen. She could not resist the temptation. She placed her hand in his. "Good, now let's see what your heart reveals."

Evergreen knew what her heart was going to reveal. It was beating louder than a jackhammer. She laughed out loud. How, how in the world was HE standing before her? Landon was thorough in his examination. No funny or sexual innuendos. He checked her ears. Told her he only saw a few dust bunnies. He placed the stethoscope between his hands and held for a few minutes. When the stethoscope encountered Evergreen's skin, it was warm to the touch. Evergreen had watched, wondering why he had held the instrument this way. What a kind gesture. Evergreen could imagine this was how the examination and conversation went with the children that he had as patients.

Landon stepped back. "Lookin' good, baby". And then he smiled the biggest, cheesiest grin she had ever seen and winked. Evergreen busted out laughing.

"Dr. Dawson, do you tell all your patients this, or am I just special?"

Landon placed his hand on Evergreen's cheek. "You have and will always be special, Evergreen Colt." The silence in the room was deafening. Time was standing still.

"Landon, I cannot do this. I will be leaving tomorrow, and I do not know when I will see you again," Evergreen explained.

"Then remember this." Landon slid his hand underneath Evergreen's hair and pulled her towards him. His lips were in the way. She could not avoid contact. Landon bit the bottom of Evergreen's lip and suckled until he felt her inhale. "Open your lips to me", Landon demanded.

"Let me taste you one more time." Evergreen did as she was told. The kiss deepened. His desire for Evergreen was beating like a storm in his chest. He could not stop it. He did not want to stop. He whispered to Evergreen, "You should be kissed as if there were no tomorrow."

CHAPTER 18

"Evergreen, Evergreen, is everything okay?" Will asked from the porch. Evergreen jumped back out of Landon's arms and reach. "I'm in here, Will. Everything is fine. Dr. Dawson has given me a clean bill of health." Will knew when he walked in that something had happened before he had walked in. What, he didn't know, but he could surmise that it was intimate enough to make Evergreen blush.

"The band, crew, and myself are packing it in for the night. Gus will be ready in the morning to pick up the tour bus."

Evergreen nodded her head in agreement. "I'll be right there, Will."

Evergreen looked at Landon. This was it. She did not know if she would ever see him again. "Landon, thank you for everything. Your kindness will never be forgotten."

"Thank you. That's it. That's all you're going to give me. Were your lips not just locked with mine? Who was I kissing?"

"You know I cannot stay. I know you cannot leave. It's just like before. You remember that day, don't you? I do. I walked into the barn to our 'spot'. I waited. I knew you had been there. I sensed it. I found what you had left me. And now, the same thing is happening to you. I cannot change my career overnight. That day, I made a promise to myself that I would never depend on another individual for my happiness. I cannot commit to anyone or anything right now. There is no easy fix to our problem. You made a choice when you left me the note. You chose your career path over our love. I will not do a repeat of the past. There can be no second time. I cannot hide or run from that day and the pain anymore. I cannot argue with you, for the decision has been taken out of our hands. I cannot turn back time, and neither can you. I cannot trust you with my heart. It was stolen the day I found the note and the rose left inside."

Evergreen looked at Landon. She loved him so much, it hurt. She knew *she* would be the one to leave this time. Evergreen kissed him as if her life depended on it. She turned and walked back to the porch where Will, Gus, and the band were finalizing the road trip for the next event. She looked one last time to see the man she loved staring with a blank look as she walked away.

Landon could not believe she had just left him standing there. What had just happened? All those years ago, she had held on to that day. Landon remembered that day. She thought he had left to pursue his career. He did not have the opportunity to tell her, he had left for her. He had left for her to realize her dreams and ambitions of becoming a country music star. Evergreen had achieved her goals. Landon had accomplished and finished his aspirations of becoming one of the top notched pediatricians in "Hopeulikit, Georgia."

The only piece of the puzzle that was missing was love, but was it, really? You know, the kind that sets your heart beating faster when you see her. The kind of love that brings a smile to your face by just talking or thinking about her. Love is an experience like no other. It takes you by surprise and leaves you feeling breathless. It is a feeling unlike anything you have known. It sneaks upon you and captures your entire soul and being. This is what Evergreen had done to Landon. His last thought as he left was, "I will never see her again."

CHAPTER 19

As in all things, life continues. There is always a hiccup every now and then. But for the most part, there is the daily routine and grind. This had been Landon for the past six months. Monday through Friday from 7 a.m. until 7 p.m., he was at Lullaby Children's Hospital. Some days were easier than others. Landon was sure that the staff had taken notice that he was more distant than before. Landon deeply cared about the treatment of his patients and their families.

When that day had occurred that he knew she had left town, he went about his normal routine at the hospital. The holidays were fast approaching. The hospital had begun pulling out the decorations and display of Christmas that would be erected during the next few days. Christmas was always huge at Lullaby Children's Hospital. The community came together to be sure that all children who must remain in the hospital due to their illness, as well as the families who lived at the hospital during this time, would have Christmas.

It was a full-blown effort on everyone's part. From having the children write letters to Santa Claus and the Christmas emergency wish list made by the families, there was no stone left unturned. All pediatricians, nurses, and staff enjoyed the feeling in the air. There was not one room Landon could walk into without realizing how blessed he was. The children, who were old enough to understand, knew that this would be where they would celebrate Christmas and HIS birth.

Landon was doing his normal rounds, when the door flew open. It was Rikkie. "Dr. Dawson, I need to speak to you now. Like ASAP." Landon told his little patient that he would return shortly and would bring a special snack just for her. She giggled and gave Landon two thumbs up. These children were resilient. They could survive the odds placed against them.

Rikkie grabbed Landon's arm. "Dr. Dawson, please listen to me. We were listening to Christmas music on the radio when he heard the news," Rikkie began. Landon looked at Rikkie with eyebrows raised, wanting to know what she was speaking about. "Dr. Dawson, it's her. There has been a serious bus crash. It was her tour bus. They are not reporting anything about the injuries of any of the occupants."

Landon stopped dead in his tracks. He grabbed Rikkie, and squeezed her arms in a vice grip. "Where, where is she?" Landon shouted. Rikkie told Landon to come to the nurses' station. She wanted to write it down on paper, so he would have all accurate information. As they approached the nurse's station, Landon saw his friend, Dr. Steele hand Rikkie the information. "Everything is on there, Landon. I wrote down the hospital, address, and telephone number."

Landon looked at Rikkie. "I have to leave. I have to catch the next flight. I'm going to head straight to the airport. Catch any flight I can that lands me close to Pinedale, Wyoming. I'll Uber from the airport and head straight there. Crispin, can you please finish my rounds for me and text me with any questions? Rikkie will be able to handle it from here. I'll let you know when I arrive," Landon hollered to Rikkie as he was racing to catch the elevator.

Rikkie had already called transportation for Landon. The young man standing outside the car raised his hand. He had been told there would be a doctor racing outside who needed to get to the airport with haste. Landon nodded and opened the passenger side door. "I need to get to the airport as quickly as possible, please." The young man could hear the urgency in the doctor's voice.

"Yes, sir. I'll have you there in less than 20 minutes." Landon thanked him and began the preparations of texting several of the staff to inform them of what was taking place, and that as soon as he landed and assessed the situation, he would call with details.

The plane landed in Pinedale, Wyoming. It seemed as if eternity had passed, when in reality it had been two hours of air travel. Landon could not get through the crowded airport quickly enough. People were everywhere. He weaved and dodged in and out, apologizing for bumping into folk as he was maneuvering through the travelers. While the plane had been unloading, Landon had taken the opportunity to call yet another Uber. Speed is what Landon needed. There was no time to waste. As the doors opened to the outside of Pinedale, Wyoming this Uber driver was ready and waiting. *Thank you, Lord, for the small things.* Landon waved his hand high in the air to capture his attention. The driver acknowledged Landon. As Landon positioned himself in the backseat and told the driver the address of the hospital, Landon recalled that he had Gus's cell phone number. He began the message with, "It's Landon, I'm in Pinedale, headed to the Big Heart General Hospital. Please tell me what is going on. How is she?" Landon did not know if Gus had been in the accident, as well, or if Gus would even have reception to receive his text. All Landon could do was pray. And pray he did.

Evergreen's last thought was that this next concert would be the last for a few months. She wasn't tired—she was completely drained, both physically and emotionally. Not only did she want to go home, she *needed* to go home. She needed her mom and dad. Evergreen needed only what a mom and dad could give a child (not just love), but guidance and advice. Evergreen had been discussing with Will the final calendar dates and destinations, when she heard Gus yell, "Brace yourself, he's gonna hit us head on." Those were the last words she heard.

The Uber driver pulled up to the hospital entrance. "I hope you find that everyone is okay, Dr. Dawson," the driver told him.

"Thank you, I appreciate it." Landon jumped out and slammed the door. He raced to get through the doors, so he could find the information desk. Landon had called the hospital while on the ride to see if information could be obtained regarding a Miss Evergreen Colt, as well as the individuals who were on the tour bus. Landon knew with privacy rules, it was a hit or miss if the hospital would share that information over the phone. The best bet was to show his credentials and ask where Evergreen had been placed upon arrival. Why did this happen? If only, and those were the words that would sustain Landon until he saw Evergreen with his own eyes.

CHAPTER 20

Evergreen could hear voices. They were all around her. The voices were unfamiliar. They were not that of Gus or Will. These were voices that were hurried with questions and answers. And there was a lot of shouting going on. Evergreen's head hurt. She did not know if it was from all the commotion or something else that was causing the pain. Evergreen could not utter one word. Her voice did not work. Evergreen could not ask where Will was. Evergreen could not move her body. Her body felt heavy. Something or someone was weighing her down.

Evergreen felt something hard placed under her back, and a tight grip was placed on her neck. She could hear scurrying about. She could not feel her hands. She could not lift her arms. This was wrong. What was happening? Her right leg was in an extreme amount of pain. She heard, rather than saw, that her leg had an object protruding from it. She would need to be rushed into surgery. Evergreen's eyes closed. She was cold. Darkness enveloped her.

Landon had his credentials already in his hand. He had been holding on to them since he had left the airport. As he approached the information desk, he presented them to the young lady behind the desk. "I am Dr. Landon Dawson, from Lullaby Children's Hospital. Can you please direct me to where the bus crash individuals have been placed?"

"Yes sir, please take the elevator to the seventh floor, where ICU is located. The nurse in charge will be able to give you information." Landon thanked her for her kindness. He could not wait for the elevators. He saw the stairwell entrance and began running, skipping steps on his way up. Time was of the essence. He could not live life without Evergreen

Colt. She made him a better person. She was the better half of Landon. She was his heartbeat.

Arriving at the entry to ICU, Landon pushed the intercom button and told them who he was. The electronic doors opened for Landon to enter. "Dr. Dawson, this way, please", he heard a voice. It was Dr. Axel Bane, a colleague of Landon's and Crispin's. "I figured you would be here. Rumor had it you guys were an item. I did not know whether to believe the tabloids or not, but evidently, there's a bit of truth to the gossip." Landon smiled.

"Evergreen Colt and I have known each other since we could walk. She had just finished a festival concert in Hopeulikit, Georgia. Can you tell me what happened?" Landon asked his colleague.

"From what I can tell, the bus driver took the impact of the hit. He's in surgery right now. I'll find out an update on him. Evergreen is also in surgery. Give me five minutes, and I'll be back with a report of her injuries and how the surgery is going. We have all the tour bus's occupants in the ER. We are in the process of examining everyone."

Landon nodded. He knew his hands were tied until details and assessment could be given. Patience was not one of Landon's strong suits. To be honest, he sucked at it. One of the nurses approached Landon. She handed him a bottled water. "If there is anything you need, Dr. Dawson, please let us know." Landon thanked her. Landon could see the nurses moving in and out of the ER rooms. He knew that there had to be at least 15 individuals on the tour bus.

Landon could not stand there and wait, and he realized where he needed to go. As Landon walked the long hallway, he could only think of how they had left things. He saw the doors. Beautiful, wooden doors with a cross in the middle. Reaching to open the door, Landon noticed how the cross split in half to allow him to walk through to what so many needed but were afraid to enter. The chapel, a sanctuary of prayer. Landon *did* believe in God. He could not *not* believe after watching the miracles that occurred every day at Lullaby Children's Hospital.

The chapel was empty. One single candle was lit. Landon took a seat in the back pew. He took a deep breath and bowed his head. His only thought was to ask, "Please do not take her from me." He sat in silence, with the glow of the candle illuminating the shadows. Landon could not lose her. She was his. She was his love, his heart, his destiny.

He heard the footsteps coming down the hallway, and he knew who it would be. He stood up. The doors opened. Dr. Axel Bane had a huge smile on his face. "She is in recovery. We had to do surgery on her leg, but she will be able to walk. She will need physical therapy to gain the strength and the mobility of the leg again."

Landon reached out to shake Dr. Bane's hand. "Thank you. There are no words to express my appreciation for what you, your staff, and the hospital have done. When can I see her?" Landon inquired.

Dr. Bane said, "We can do so now."

Landon stopped, "And Gus. Is Gus okay?"

"He is. He is also in recovery. Most of his injuries were to his head. Lacerations, stitches, and concussion. He will recover. We are keeping both of them for a few days for observation."

Again, Landon began the walk down the long hallway to where he would be taken to ICU recovery. Landon had not given thought to what he would say. As they approached ICU, Landon stopped before entering. One more prayer. There was always a need for one more prayer.

"She's in Room 2. I do not know if she is awake and alert, but you are more than welcome to go in."

Landon nodded his understanding of the situation. He was as quiet as a church mouse. Before he sat, he walked to where Evergreen was. He reviewed the monitor readings. Landon knew better than to read the patient's charts. He was *not* her doctor. Landon sat down in the chair next to her bed and reached for Evergreen's hand. As soft as a warm summer breeze, he entwined his fingers to hers. Landon did not want to admit it. He was tired. The quickness with which he had to react and do everything in such haste and manner had taken its toll. He closed his eyes and lay his head on top of their hands. Just a few minutes was all that was needed.

Landon could feel movement in his hair. He was not fully awake. The slight rubbing of his hair in a circular motion felt relaxing. Landon attempted to open his eyes. And then it dawned on him. Evergreen was making the circular motion in his hair. He quickly placed her hand against his lips. The kiss had the desired effect.

Evergreen mumbled, "Where did you come from? And, aren't you supposed to be working?" Yes, his Evergreen was back. Still questioning his whereabouts.

"I saw on the news that there had been a bus crash and all crash victims had been brought here. What did you think I was going to do? Wait until you called me? That would have been a few weeks from the looks of ya!"

Evergreen smiled. "Are you okay, Landon?"

"Evergreen Colt, I am just fine. It's you I am worried about. If you don't feel like talking, I understand. I am not going anywhere. I'll be right here. Get some rest." Landon stood up and kissed Evergreen on the forehead. She whispered the words he had longed to hear. He knew it was the anesthesia that was causing this.

Evergreen knew she needed to hold on to Landon's hand. She was not going to let him go. She needed him. She made sure he could not remove his hand from her grasp. Landon relaxed. She was spunky. She was going to be alright. With physical therapy and following strict instructions from Dr. Bane, Evergreen would resume life as normal. Landon leaned his head back on the chair. Just a few minutes to rest.

Landon heard the nurse enter the room. "Sorry, Dr. Dawson, we need to check her vitals." Landon acknowledged that he understood. When she finished, he opened his mouth, and before he could ask, the nurse informed him that all vitals looked good and for him to continue to rest.

Landon felt, rather than saw, the sun. It was peeping through the hospital room curtains. It was going to be a glorious day. He rose to open the blinds and see if Evergreen needed anything. She was stirring in the bed and moaning. It was her leg. He knew the sound of pain. He pushed the nurse's button to bring attention to Evergreen's room. The preparation began as soon as her assigned nurse walked in. Vitals, pain meds, changing of IV fluids – nurses were the unsung heroes. As Evergreen sat up in the bed, she rubbed her eyes with both her hands. She looked down at her leg, which had been casted from the thigh to her foot. Without knowing why, she started crying. Not little tears, but big, alligator tears. Landon rushed to the bed and pulled her to his chest.

"Hey, what happened? It's going to be okay. What can I do?"

Evergreen sniffled and rubbed her nose against his shoulder. "I'm just overwhelmed. We have bookings for festivals and concerts. How will I tell my fans? How can I reschedule?" Landon knew she was feeling blue, and it seemed the odds were against her.

"We will take one second, one minute, one hour, one day at a time. Nod with me, so I know you're not being hard-headed, Evergreen Colt."

Evergreen was thankful she had Landon. He had been an important part of her life as a child and into the young adult years. Here he stood, ready to tackle the obstacles with her.

And that's what Landon decided they would do. Landon called Lullaby Children's Hospital and spoke to his friend and colleague, Dr. Crispin Steele, to inform him of days that he would be off for personal leave.

CHAPTER 21

Landon took the time to get an AirBNB close to the hospital where Evergreen was recuperating. She was doing well and would be transferred to the rehab facility in a few days. Landon had been in and out during the weeks that Evergreen, Gus, the band members and production crew had been in the hospital. Most had been released within 24 to 48 hours. Gus was going through rehab as well, and made a great therapy buddy for Evergreen. Gus would egg Evergreen on to do more than him because, of course, she was younger, and he didn't want to show her up.

Will had stopped in, just as Landon knew he would. When this happened, Landon would step out of Evergreen's room and give them the privacy they needed. During these moments, Landon would head to the cafeteria. He had become friends with several of the doctors, as well as nursing staff. All had been welcoming and more than happy to take him under their wing and share their favorite spots of their town.

Landon was backing into Evergreen's room, when he heard sobbing. He was returning from the cafeteria, where he had found that they had Vanilla Cokes – Evergreen's favorite and his, too. He situated the drinks down on the table. Tears flooded Evergreen's eyes and spilled down her cheeks. "What has happened? I've only been gone for a few minutes, sweetheart," Landon rushed to comfort her.

"It's Will. He's left. He had to return back to the office. He needs to handle the other artists and their schedules. We had a discussion. Both he and I came to the realization that I would need a new manager to finish out the rest of the season. We also spoke about our relationship. We have both known for a while that it would never develop past the point of just being dear friends. It's so much at one time, and yet, it needed to happen. It should have happened earlier than this, but we kept putting off "the talk." I don't know if I am crying because of relief, or because I know this chapter in my life has been closed. I'm just feeling emotional today. I will be leaving rehab and headed back on the road."

Landon had followed everything that Evergreen had said. And she had said a lot in just a few short minutes. He heard Will had left and then, he heard the words "headed back on the road."

"Like the devil, you will. Evergreen Colt, you are not going back on the road," Landon stated with fierce determination.

Evergreen knew he would react this way. There was no tip-toeing around her career and what was expected. The path she had chosen was her journey. No one else's. "Landon, I will be leaving here in two weeks. I will head home to rest, and then, I will hit the road again. I've cancelled several events, so I can recuperate. But both you and I know if I am not in the public's eye, then I will fade. My career demands it."

Landon could not believe his ears. She could not be serious. She was not ready to hit the road again. Time to gain her strength and to rest from the surgery was needed and required. He was going to put his foot down. He may need to put both feet down. Evergreen Colt was in for a rude awakening regarding her career, and Landon Dawson was just the man to bring her back to reality.

"I forbid it, Evergreen. You are going home. You are going to sit on your cute hiney and be like a bump on a pickle – you are just going to sit there. This is not up for discussion. This is what is going to happen."

"All that in one breath, Dr. Dawson, I am impressed," Evergreen smiled.

"I'm not smiling, Evergreen. Taking care of yourself and following your doctor's orders are critical to your healing," Landon commented.

Evergreen laughed. "And this is where the road splits, Dr. Dawson. The last time I checked, you were *not* my doctor; it's Dr. Axel Bane. If he gives me two thumbs up after rehab and physical therapy, I'll be packing sooner than later. And that's all that needs to be discussed. Are we clear, Dr. Dawson?"

Lord, she was stubborn. Landon had forgotten how hardheaded she was until this very moment, but the memory was coming back to him. "We shall see, Evergreen. We shall see."

CHAPTER 22

For the past three weeks, she knew he would be on time. Landon Dawson had a few faults, but one of them was not being late. Actually, Landon arrived early to every physical therapy appointment. Evergreen was getting stronger each day. Evergreen did not want Landon to know that she looked forward to physical therapy because he was there. He was so supportive and encouraging. When she felt like she could not lift her leg any higher or extend it any further, he would tease her until she would do the exercise, just to prove him wrong.

She knew she needed to tell Landon that she had talked to Gus and the band. They would be packing and leaving to begin a small concert tour the first of December for the Christmas holidays. Evergreen knew this would not go well. She saw Landon walk through the office door. "Everything good. Ready for your last day. Let's hit it and get it." Evergreen loved when he said "hit it and get it". She knew he did not want to waste time, and she knew there was never a time like the present.

"Landon, I will be joining the band in two weeks. Dr. Bane has given me his blessing, and I will be released today, as a matter of fact. Before you even open your mouth to argue with me, it's not up for discussion. It's going to happen, Landon. I just wanted you to hear from me first."

It was as if someone had punched Landon in the stomach. He had known this day was coming. He just did not realize he would feel the way he did. He looked at Evergreen as she finished. Just as he had done, that one day so long ago, he walked towards Evergreen. He pulled her into his embrace and kissed her. Too much had passed between them.

It could not be repaired. The damage had been done, and the sooner Landon moved on, the better it would be for both.

That morning before Landon left to attend Evergreen's physical therapy appointment, Landon was one step closer to telling Evergreen the truth. He wanted to tell her the truth of why he had left. The true reason behind the note and the rose he had left that one fateful day. A day that would begin their journey. Landon never got the opportunity to reveal his feelings, nor to tell Evergreen the story of the rose. The note had begun the journey for both.

"Evergreen, I am not going to argue with you or even plead with you not to go back on the road. I can see your mind is made up. I pray that you will find what you have been searching for all these years." Landon turned and grabbed the handle of the office door. He looked back at Evergreen staring at him. He knew things would never be the same again. He knew this was the last time they would see each other face to face.

Landon walked out into the fresh air from the medical office. He stopped and paused and allowed the sun to warm his entire being. It felt comfortable, like a warm fuzzy blanket. It was time to go home. It was time to return to his career and his patients. The holidays were just around the corner. This was his favorite time of the year. This was a month that belonged to the children, especially at Lullaby Children's Hospital. Landon was headed to the airport. Telephone calls needed to be made.

Evergreen could not say anything. Landon knew. She would not give up her dream. She could not look back and think what if, should I, could I, would I? Evergreen was at the peak of her country music career. Once you stopped, you were forgotten. That was the plain and simple truth of the industry. Social media, public relations, and marketing were the three keys to being successful. There was no denying that long hours, being on the road, and sleepless nights were part of an artist's life. Evergreen knew if she stopped now, it would be more difficult to get back in the swing of things and to climb the mountain one more time to maintain being on top. She watched Landon exit through the medical office doors. She knew this was the last time they would see each other face to face.

CHAPTER 23

There was a saying that time stands still for no one. This had never been truer than when Landon returned to Lullaby Children's Hospital. It was the end of fall and the beginning of winter. Changes were being made at the hospital to accommodate the holidays. Halloween had come and gone. In the blink of an eye, Thanksgiving had dropped by and decorations for Christmas were being put in place for the big celebration for the children and families of Lullaby.

Landon was glad for this fact. He had chosen not to reflect on that day that he turned to leave Evergreen. When he had returned to the hospital, several of the staff had asked how she was. Landon had told them she had recuperated enough to continue her concert schedule. There was no fluff and puff about Evergreen or how he felt. Landon had kept his feelings to himself. After his answers had been short and curt, the staff knew better than to dig further.

Crispin would make a few comments to the side to get a rise out of Landon, but Landon would not bite. Landon had told Crispin that it was meant to be, and he was not looking back. Crispin told Landon, "But you're not looking forward, either. It's like you've hit stalemate and you've just given up." Landon had shrugged off the comment, because he knew it was the truth. If Landon could just get through Christmas and be able to return home, he knew he would feel better. Just a few more days.

Evergreen had hit the road hard. She became more determined than ever to make the top 10 on the country music charts and to promote "Stolen Roses" to the number one song. This had become the number one song that fans requested. At first, Evergreen did not want to make it known as such. The fans would chant the words "Stolen Roses" at the concerts.

Evergreen had one more gig that she had been requested to make. It was a guest appearance for the Christmas holidays. It was Lullaby Children's Hospital, Landon's hospital. She had told the band, the crew, and Gus that she would be sure that they would be home for the holidays to spend them with family and friends. All were excited for the last show of the season.

Evergreen had made sure that everyone had overnight accommodations before they arrived for the last gig at the children's hospital. This was her Christmas gift to them. It was a beautiful bed and breakfast. It was a home that was colonial in style. Evergreen had tried The Dreamer Bed and Breakfast. They were booked. But Miss TeeTee gave Evergreen Miss Betty's number. Evergreen had spoken to the Miss Betty and told her they would take the entire bed and breakfast from Friday night through Sunday morning. Miss Betty was thrilled to have the home to full capacity. When the tour bus pulled up, it was if a picture from *Country Is Us* magazine had been torn from the pages. The driveway was lit on both sides with beautiful white lights. The porch was lined with poinsettias. The white columns were trimmed in green garland highlighted with white lights intertwined. As Evergreen and the crew exited the bus and stepped on the pavement, you could tell cookies were baking. Everyone stopped and smiled. There was nothing like the scent of baking, especially during Christmas.

Evergreen sat in her room. She just needed a moment to breathe. She needed a brief respite from all the hustle and bustle of getting in their rooms and getting situated and being introduced to the owner. Miss Betty (as she told Evergreen and the rest to call her) was so welcoming. Miss Betty got everyone acclimated to their rooms and gave a quick tour and itinerary of breakfast, lunch, and supper timeframes. Evergreen knew the band would, more than likely, go sit outside on the deck. The fire pit had been placed in the middle, to give warmth for those who wanted to brave the outdoors. Laughter could be heard into Evergreen's window. She could rest a bit. All was right with the world.

Landon woke up. Today was Saturday. He wanted to get to the hospital to help with the festivities. Saturdays were normally his day off. Typically, Landon would wake up and head to the gym for about an hour workout, head home to shower, watch sports on television, make a call or two to family, and snack throughout the day. Lately, though, Landon would spend most of the weekend by himself.

He had to admit it. He was in the Christmas spirit. He could not wait to see the children and how their eyes sparkled when the lighting of the Christmas tree countdown began. The atrium of the hospital looked like a winter wonderland. And of course, the best was when Santa walked through the entrance of the hospital. All eyes were glued to him. Landon had dressed casually, in his favorite pink Henley, jeans, a jacket, and his cowboy boots.

Evergreen woke to the smell of bacon frying. She could hear voices in the kitchen. All exuberant. As she walked into the kitchen, she saw Miss Betty at the stove. She was cracking eggs open, flipping pancakces, and buttering toast, all the while turning the bacon. Evergreen was in heaven. This was how breakfast should be. Evergreen didn't even know if there was room for her, because it looked as if all chairs were taken. Gus saw her and motioned to her to come sit beside him. Evergreen made her way to the empty spot.

Miss Betty began placing the food on the table. She smacked Gus's hand when he went to reach for the hot biscuit. "Gus, we need to pray over the meal." Gus nodded.

"Sorry about that Miss Betty," Gus smiled and, then, winked at her. Evergreen saw that interaction. Something was happening here. What? Evergreen did not know, but it was time that Gus spread his wings. Evergreen liked Miss Betty. She was a good match for Gus. As they sat at the table discussing the event and the songs to play and placing them in a set, Evergreen had to admit to herself that she was a bit nervous. It was not like this was twenty thousand people attending one of her concerts. These were children and their families who could not leave the hospital. What was it that the hospital event coordinator told her… it would be a blessing if she could spare just one or two hours of her time. There was no way that Evergreen could turn that down. And like the coordinator told her, just one or two hours. What could go wrong? That she may sing longer than anticipated or he may be there.

Evergreen looked at everyone at the table and cleared her throat. "Before we leave, I want to take this moment to tell you how much this day and what you are giving back to the children mean. You have given your time and yourself. I could not ask for a better group of folks to share this day with than you. I love each of you forever and a day."

Gus stood up. "Well, only one thing left to do."

The band and production crew looked at Gus. All at the same time shouted, "Let's hit it and git it."

Landon had arrived at Lullaby Children's Hospital. The day was cold. A light breeze was in the air, with just a hint of flurries floating around. Landon walked through the hospital entrance. The entire first floor, where the atrium was located, was hustle and bustle. Landon could see that several of the staff had decided to come in on their day off to help with decorations and putting up the Christmas tree. This is why Landon loved Lullaby Children's Hospital: everyone cared. Everyone knew the true meaning of Christmas and that Christmas was for the children.

Landon decided that since he was already at the hospital, he may as well check on his patients. Walking to the elevator, his thoughts returned to the day she had told him she was going back on the road. He could not help but wonder which city she would be in for the holidays. The doors opened to Landon's floor. No matter which floor you were visiting, all children's rooms were decorated either on the outside or inside. The nurses' stations were never empty of candy and cookies. It was as if the smell of vanilla and gingerbread had invaded the hospital. Every floor had a tree specifically designated in a theme. There was a sports tree, a cooking tree, a princess tree, a pet tree – if a child could think of a theme, the staff made sure one was completed. Landon made his way down the hallway, checking in with the families and patients. He enjoyed speaking with the children and asking what they had asked Santa to bring them for Christmas.

As he was leaving and heading back to the nurses' station to check in with them, the Christmas music resonated throughout the floor. Landon loved this time of year. There was thanks for the ending of the year and faith and hope for the beginning of the new. Landon did not know who the hospital had procured for entertainment for this weekend, but they were pretty dang good. Whoever the female was singing, had a beautiful voice. As far as he could tell, she was pretty on-key with her tone. As he arrived at the nurses' station, he could tell they had felt the effects of the Christmas music as well. He saw Rikkie and knew if anyone knew the goings on of the weekend and what events were taking place, it was her.

"Rikkie, who did we get this year for entertainment?" Landon inquired.

Rikkie shook her head. "I don't know. She just arrived, and we've not had time to go to the atrium." Landon felt, rather than knew, something was up. Rikkie looked like the Cheshire cat. She could not stop smiling. "I think you definitely need to check it out and, then, let us know what you think. We have all the patients charted for the morning. Plus, you're not supposed to be here."

"Fine. I'll go scope it out and then let you know if I approve."

Rikkie grinned. "Oh, I'm pretty sure you will approve."

Landon nodded his head in confirmation. "I'll be gone for just ten minutes. Page me if you need anything." Landon pushed the down button for the elevators. As the doors closed, the last words Landon heard were, "He's gonna be so surprised."

CHAPTER 24

The elevator doors opened to the atrium. Landon could see that the rocking chairs had been gathered and pushed into a circle for the parents and children. Studies had shown that rocking was relaxing for both mothers and babies who were a bit overwhelmed with emotions and adjustment of a newborn (especially during the holiday season). Lullaby Children's Hospital had placed rocking chairs throughout the facility.

From Landon's point of view, all he could see was that the singer was in the middle of the group on the floor. He walked towards the group to get a better look. Grammie was on the outside of her welcome booth. She grabbed Landon's elbow. "Stop being a fool and apologize. Love is not soft and fuzzy. It is a strength you find within yourself to give of yourself. Sometimes, you need to let go of you, so you can see what has always been."

Landon looked at Grammie. She had clearly been drinking too much eggnog or eating too much sugar. Maybe both. *Apologize for what?* Landon thought to himself. He maneuvered through the children, inching closer to see who was in the middle. He heard a small child's voice ask, "Will you please sing ………..for us?"

Who was it? What song did the child request? Landon could not hear. Why were these parents and children not parting, so Landon could get a better glance? And then the female singer replied, "I would love to sing 'Stolen Roses.'"

Landon froze. Time stopped. There was no way this could be happening. He had resigned himself to the fact that it was never meant to be. When he returned to the hospital, he did not share what had taken place with anyone. She had moved on. She had moved on without him. The sooner he accepted it, the better off he would be. And that's what he had done. He had accepted it. Evergreen Colt was not a part of his life, nor his future.

As soon as she and the band had arrived, they had been welcomed with hugs, kisses on the cheek, and a slew of Merry Christmas wishes. Evergreen was glad that this event would end her tour for the year. This was exactly what she needed. Evergreen knew with the crowd that had gathered of families and their children that sitting in the middle was the best spot. The band had decided not to set up. They knew that sometimes, loud noises could affect the children who could be sensitive. They stood to the side. Evergreen looked over at them. They were all beaming with joy. Yes, this holiday event was definitely the best of the tour season.

It was a given, at all concerts and events, her #1 song was always requested. When the little girl had asked her to sing it, Evergreen felt something in the air. Something was about to happen. Evergreen closed her eyes and sang "Pull me closer…Giving me a reason to stay…Sometimes, it ain't easy.…But easy would just be a lie…Light me up, let's not end like these stolen roses…You stole from our love…" When she had finished the first chorus, Evergreen opened her eyes. He was standing there. Just like before, when she had seen him at the festival concert. She continued the song. Evergreen could not take her eyes off him. A tear formed in the corner of her eye. She could not stop it. It trickled down her cheek. She could not wipe it away. When the song was finished, the entire atrium was cheering, applauding, and a few were rubbing their eyes.

Evergreen could not stand up. He was walking towards her. He was getting closer. He placed his hand for her to reach. He pulled her up from the middle of the atrium floor. And then, in front of God and everybody, he kissed her with such passion that Evergreen was oblivious to the *oooohhhhs* and *aaaaaahhhhs*.

Landon did not know what came over him. The only thing that mattered was that he needed to get to Evergreen, and no one or nothing was going to stand in his way. Everything that Landon had felt since he had written the note consumed him. And then, it came to him. He was and had been in love with Evergreen Colt all of his life. Could she forgive him? Could he make her understand why he had left? As the old adage says, there is no time like the present.

Evergreen did not want Landon to pull away. The passion in that kiss was boundless. Could Landon recognize the plain and simple truth? Did he know the depth of her love for him?

Landon heard the crowd hooping and hollering and applauding. They had become the center of attention. The little girl who had requested the song ran up to Evergreen. Evergreen stepped back and knelt down, eye to eye with the little girl. She squealed with excitement, and Evergreen gave her a hug and kiss and thanked her for requesting her song. The little girl turned around and said, "Pretty please, may I have your autograph on my t-shirt?" Landon laughed. The little girl was just so sweet and cute – who could turn that request down? Landon and Evergreen watched as the little girl skipped back to her mom. She turned and screamed to the crowd, "Do you see, do you see – she signed my t-shirt." Evergreen was happy that she was able to bring a smile to the little girl.

Landon had moved to observe and to watch the exchange with the little girl Evergreen. When Evergreen stood up, he inquired if she could step away with him. He promised to return her to the atrium and the children. Over to the side, where the Christmas tree had been put up, was a secret little nook where the mistletoe hung for that special occasion.

"I have to tell you something, Evergreen. And you need to listen. Don't interrupt me. Let me get all of it out before you come to a decision. I ask only that you listen."

Evergreen nodded in agreement.

"That day when I left the note with the rose was the most difficult choice I have ever made. I knew that if I did not leave, you would not leave. I also knew of your dream to become a country music artist and travel to share your gift of songwriting. From the moment I became aware of the dream, I knew what needed to be done. The note and the rose were not meant to be a goodbye. It was meant to be a prayer for your success and for you to take on your journey. Along the way, I came to the conclusion that I have and will continue to love you with each breath I take. I cannot deny it any longer. I had hoped that you could see yourself through my eyes. If you only knew how those moments we shared mattered so much to me."

Evergreen placed two fingers on his lips. "Stop, Landon. Just stop. You are the reason why I became stronger. You are the reason why I have held on to this." Landon watched as Evergreen placed her hand in back pocket jeans and pulled out a white piece of paper. She began to unfold it. Inside the note, Landon saw it. Pieces of the rose were laid perfectly inside the paper. It was THE note and THE rose Landon had left for Evergreen.

"Now you know, Landon. My #1 song was written for you. The song reflects the love I have always had for you. The rose, the journey, the song – my love is yours. I may not have gone where I intended to go, but the journey of the rose has brought me to where I need to be. Here with you."

Landon could not help but smile. "Are you saying what I think you're saying, Evergreen Colt? Because if you are, I am here to tell you, I am head over heels, ain't no denying it, in love with you, and will always be."

Evergreen placed her arms around Landon. "In every song I have written, I have placed a piece of you. I am never going to let you go. I will love you until my heart stops."

Landon looked into Evergreen's eyes. He knew that this was love.

Love was….the rose….the journey…the song – it was "Stolen Roses".

DE DE COX

"Born and raised in Rooster Run, Kentucky, Deanna (de de) Cox, grew up reading romance novels. She and her sister, Casonya, would discuss the books and ponder what they would write, if the opportunity ever arose. At the age of 30, de de began to write her first romance book. But as in life, circumstances change and life moves you in a different direction. The direction led de de into the charitable industry, due to the upbringing of her Grandma Bea. She is actively involved in Make a Wish Foundation, Blessings in a Backpack, Spalding University, Toys for Tots, The Molly Johnson Foundation, Indiana Bulldog Rescue Foundation and volunteers with numerous other charities. She is a prelim director in the festival and America pageant system. She is also the Executive Co-Director of the Miss Kentucky Junior High, High School and Collegiate America state pageant. At the mature age of 35, her only child was born, Isaiah Bo. His name is taken from Isaiah 40:31. Bo is the actual cover model for the books *Two Degrees One Heart, the Perfect Chrystmas and now, Two Degrees Hotter*. When de de began writing the book, she had no idea she would have a son, and never imagined Bo would be on the cover - a book she had written before he was even born. de de feels that everything is in God's timing. Her second son, Matthew Tracy, came into her life to complete her family. She has been married to Scott Cox, her best friend from high school, for over 30 years. We are a society that impatiently waits for patience. de de continues her passion of writing romance books, for where would the world be without love? Never forget Acts 20:35."